Fire & Fury

An Endless Winter Novel

Book 4

By

Theresa Shaver

Also by Theresa Shaver

Chapter One - Skylar

When we reach the closed gates of the summer camp, Rex jumps out of the truck and is joined by Marsh from my dad's truck. There is nothing but silence inside the vehicle while we watch them in the headlights as they push the gates open. No one is celebrating the arrival at our new home because we're all a little shell-shocked by what went down tonight. Ben and Matty are asleep, curled up with each other against the back door. Jackson, lost in his grief, is in the middle and Joslin is beside him staring ahead with an empty expression on her face. Lance, Rex and I rode in the front seat with Ethan. Marsh, Sasha, and Belle rode in my dad's truck.

Once the guys get the gates open, Lance drives through and swings the truck toward a large building off to the right. It's so dark out here that I only get brief glimpses of other small buildings as the headlight beams wash over them. He parks the truck pointing at the front of the large building so that the headlights light up the entrance and shuts the engine off. Ethan pulls up beside us, adding the light from the smaller truck.

Lance turns to me before quickly glancing into the back seat at the others and then looks back at me.

"You guys hang tight for a few minutes while we get some lights on inside. I put out some lanterns that we brought earlier today but I don't want to mess with the generator until we have daylight in the morning." When no one responds to him, he sighs. "We'll leave the unloading for tonight and just get some sleeping areas set up. It's been a long day."

More silence greets him so he just opens the door and gets out joining Ethan, Rex, and Marsh. I watch until they disappear through the entrance and then close my eyes. I have so many conflicting emotions flooding through me right now and I need to try and get a handle on them before I start interacting with the others, especially Joslin. Right now I'm torn between hating her for destroying AIRIA and gratitude for getting us away from what would have been a brutal life under my Uncle Bill. I want to be happy that we have this new place that Lance and Marsh claim is amazing and a huge stockpile of supplies to help us get started but the loss of my home and AIRIA has tainted it.

I had come to accept that Ben and I would leave the bunker to work on building a new life before the soldiers came but I always thought I would have AIRIA and the bunker to go back to if things didn't work out in the world. Now that my security blanket has not only been taken away but shredded and burned to ash, I'm terrified.

A knock on the window beside my head brings me back to my surroundings with a flinch and I see Rex's inquiring face on the other side of the glass. He uses his thumb to point toward the building so I nod and unbuckle my seatbelt and twist around to the back seat. I let my eyes skim past Joslin and Jackson until they land on the two sleeping boys, reach back and gently shake them awake. I have to force an uplifting tone into my voice when they blink owlishly at me.

"Come on, sleepyheads. Let's go check out our new home!"

I twist back around and push open my door before jumping down and opening theirs. I help them both down from the high truck cab and pass a sleepy Matty to Rex to help steady him. Once Ben is on his feet, I reach back up to close the door and make eye contact with Joslin. She and Jackson haven't made any move to leave the truck. They look so lost and alone sitting there. No matter how I feel right now about her and what she's done, they are both with us now and we'll have to find a way to make it work. Jackson doesn't even seem to be on the planet with us so I start with him.

"Hey, Jackson! Jackson!" His eyes blink a few times and his head slowly turns my way. I hold back a wince from the complete devastation I see in his eyes and push forward.

"Hey, there. I need you to come with me. Come out of the truck, Jackson. Come with me and I'll take you somewhere you can lay down and sleep. Ok?"

He jerks his head in agreement and slides toward me so I step back out of the way so he can get down. I don't really know what more to say to him right now but thankfully, Ethan steps up beside me and takes the guy's arm and leads him toward the building. I watch them for a few seconds before turning back to the open truck door. Joslin has slid over and she's hovering half in, half out of the truck when we lock eyes again she starts talking.

"Skylar...I just want to say..."

I cut her off mid-sentence. "No, not now. Tomorrow we can talk. I need some time first."

She nods sadly and looks away as she slides the rest of the way out of the truck and shuts the door. I turn toward the building and see Rex and the boys disappearing through the door so I dash ahead and leave her to follow. I know I'll have to talk to her eventually about what happened tonight but I'm just not ready. I don't know if I really ever will be.

I enter the building and take a look around but it's just your standard plain lobby so I move down a hallway that has lit lanterns every six feet or so. There are rooms off of the hallway but the lantern light doesn't penetrate them so I just pass them by. Tomorrow will be soon enough to explore. I follow the hallway to the end where I can hear the sound of voices and step into a large open space.

There are lanterns placed all around the huge room and I find myself looking up to the domed glass ceiling that covers the area. With the lanterns on, the glass acts like a mirror and reflects the light back. I can only imagine how much work it's going to be to clean seven years worth of dirt and grime from the glass in order to let the sun shine through so we can grow plants in here. Again, something to worry about tomorrow.

I catch sight of Rex and the boys off to the left so I head toward them and see a nest of blankets with a few pillows set up. I drop to my knees beside Rex and start pulling the boots from Ben's feet before guiding him under the blankets and tucking him in for the night. Matty crawls in beside him and once again they snuggle up together like puppies and are asleep almost instantly. I sigh in relief that they're too exhausted to ask all the questions I'm sure they have about this new place.

I push myself to my feet and look around the large room to get my bearings and see that other nests have been created for sleeping. Belle and Sasha have already laid down and next to them, just a few feet away, Ethan is kneeling in front of Jackson and coaxing him down to the floor where he drapes a blanket over him. I keep turning in a circle until I noticed Joslin standing in the entryway, still looking hesitant. I turn away from her before she sees me looking in her direction and lean toward Rex.

"Can you help her, please? I just can't…deal with her yet."

He looks over toward the entry to the room and sees her standing there before giving my arm a squeeze. "Yeah of course. I'll take care of it. Why don't you lay down with the boys and get some sleep? We're going to have a lot of work to do tomorrow and it's already pretty late."

I lean forward and rest my head against his shoulder for a second.

"Thank you, Rex," I whisper. "Thank you for everything. I don't know if I could… I mean, AIRIA…Benny…" My voice chokes off as grief swamps me.

He wraps his arms around me and pulls me against him in a hug and whispers into my hair. "I'm here for you Skylar, I'm here for all of it. Don't worry about Benny. I'll help you. I'll help you with everything. We will keep him safe and will build something real here. Something to be proud of."

With a last squeeze, he lets me go and pushes to his feet and heads toward Joslin. I let him handle her and crawl into the blankets with the boys, pulling both of them close to me and close my eyes. I want to escape in sleep but my mind won't stop going round and round with all the memories I have of AIRIA and my lost home. There are so many "what if's" that I circle around on how I could have done things differently to maybe change the outcome of what happened. I lay there for hours after I hear Rex join us on the other side of the boys but no answers come to me. I finally just give up on second-guessing and start to accept the changes in mine and Ben's life as the darkness of the room starts to brighten. It's then that I finally find the escape of sleep I was looking for.

Chapter Two - Skylar

When I open my eyes next it's to the sun shining down on me. Even through the dirty, dusty windows of the atrium, it feels glorious. I stretch my stiff body, my muscles are sore from sleeping on the hard concrete floor with nothing but a blanket to provide padding and reach for Ben. The blanket beside me is heaped into a pile and there's no sign of either of the two boys that I fell asleep with. Rex is missing too so I assume he's taking care of them but when I sit up and look around the room I see that I'm the only one in it.

I quickly push to my feet and follow the hallway and the smell of oatmeal in the air. I start checking doors randomly until I come to the one with a kitchen behind it. Belle and Sasha are the only ones in there and they are stacking the food we brought from my pantry onto shelves. I step deeper into the room and rub my eyes just as Belle turns to reach into a half-empty bin. When she sees me, a sweet smile crosses her face and she comes rushing over to me.

"Skylar there you are! Oh sweetie, you look so tired. Rex said that you didn't sleep much last night so we let you rest." She reaches out and grabs my hands, peering down at them with a frown. "How are you feeling? Are your hands still hurting you?"

I stiffen in surprise but force myself to stand still with my hands resting in hers as she studies the healing palms. I gradually relax and let her warmth and kindness wash over me. I haven't had a real conversation with Belle since the day she helped me get ready for our party in my bathroom. I had forgotten just how kind and caring she is.

I close my hands around hers and give them a small squeeze. "I'm okay Belle. My hands are healing nicely but I am a little bit tired. I had a lot to process last night so it took me a while to fall asleep." I look past her and notice Sasha has stopped stacking food and is now watching us. I take in everything they've managed to stack on shelves so far and wince. "Wow, it sure felt like we brought a whole lot more last night while we were clearing the shelves of my pantry."

Belle lets go of my hands and turns to the side to wrap one arm around my shoulders and takes in the shelves as well. She gives a little laugh. "We've barely scratched the surface, honey. Sasha and I have been bringing in the bins ourselves because we lost our heavy lifters first thing this morning so we haven't made a whole lot of progress."

I lift my eyebrows in confusion. "Oh? Where's everybody at then?"

She gives my shoulder another squeeze and then drops her arm and heads back to the bin they were unloading to keep emptying it as she talks.

"Well, the men were up first thing this morning grumbling about sleeping on concrete so they went out to check all the cabins and decided that most of the mattresses in there are useless. So they unloaded the cargo truck and drove it over to some resort that's nearby to scavenge new ones as well as more bedding. They left a stack of the supplies in front of the door outside that Sasha and I have been bringing in bit by bit."

I stiffen in concern at that. "They took Benny and Matty on a scavenging run?" I ask in a sharp tone.

Belle looks up at me with a frown and shakes her head. "No of course not! The boys are outside entertaining themselves with the cow and chickens. Don't worry, Joslin's watching over them."

I don't even bother replying to that. I just spin on my heel and storm out of the room down the hallway and out the main doors. I'm looking in every direction but freeze when I hear Ben's high-pitched squeal of laughter and zero in on him. I want to be angry that the boys have been left with Joslin, who I don't consider a real part of our group, but it's hard to keep that feeling when I see the look of pure joy on my little brother's face as she pushes him on a swing for the very first time.

It brings back memories of when I was small and my mother would push me on the swing. The thrill and rush of happiness to soar back and forth while clutching the chains is a unique childhood must that my brother never got. I let the anger go and slowly walk over to the play structure on the opposite side of the yard. I feel a laugh bubbling up in my chest when Matty zooms down the slide with an almost perfect replica of Marsh's trademark rebel yell. This is what I wanted for Ben. A life under the sun where he could run and play and laugh with his best friend. The loss of the bunker and AIRIA dims slightly at the sound of their laughter.

"Sky, Sky! Look at me! Look at how high I'm going!" He yells in delight when he sees me coming. I let the smile grow bigger on my face at the pure joy he's feeling. Matty dashes toward me and skids to a stop.

"Can you push me on the other swing? I want to fly too!" He begs.

I start nodding my head but Joslin speaks up.

"I'll push you, Matty. Let's let Skylar push her brother for a bit first."

It's kindness and understanding that I see in her eyes before she quickly looks away and moves over to the next swing in the row as Matty whoops out his agreement. I have so many conflicting feelings about this girl but I still don't want to deal with them yet so I just move into position behind Ben and give him a light push to keep him swinging. Soon Matty is pumping his legs and they're both flying in tandem. I let myself relax in the repetitive motion and start to look around between pushes. I'm getting my first real look at the camp after coming here last night in the darkness and I like what I see.

The large double gates are closed, leaving us secured with the wall running all the way around the camp. I count eight small cabins and two other buildings besides the main one we slept in last night. I can see Nods tethered like a dog to a post that has a bare metal ring on it that once must have been a basketball hoop. There's a mound of hay spread out around her and she seems happy enough. There's no sign of the chickens but I can hear their squawking now and again so they must be around here somewhere. I feel bad knowing that I didn't tend to them myself last night but I'm grateful someone took care of it. My eyes land on the pile of bins and supplies that we had filled the truck with sitting in front of the main building waiting to be put away. I wince at the reminder of all the work that needs to be done that I'm shirking.

I stop pushing Ben and let him slow down. "Ok, guys. Break time is over! We have a lot of work to do to get this place set up and I'm going to need your help."

Both boys jump from the swing seats and nod eagerly. I beam at them proudly. They've both missed out on a lot of normal childhood activities in their short lives but they never hesitate to lend a hand when work needs to be done. They're such good boys. All four of us head toward the stack of supplies just as Belle and Sasha come out of the building to grab another bin. When we meet up with them, I point at the stack.

"I'm not sure which ones have the meat and other perishables we took from the fridge and freezer last night but they need to be done next or we could lose a bunch to thawing. We need to cook, can, dehydrate or smoke everything we can before we lose it."

Joslin clears her throat and steps forward. "Actually, we should be able to keep it the way it is." When we all just stare at her she continues. "In one of the truckloads that came here in the last few days were some boxes with solar panels, batteries, and inverters. Once the guys get back we can hook them up to get the freezers and fridge working but until then we should take them inside and put them somewhere that's cool so they last as long as possible."

I look away from her back toward the pile considering everything we brought and ask, "How much power can we get from what you had sent over?"

She lifts her hands up in front of her and looks down at them before shaking her head and dropping them back to her sides. "Sorry, I'm used to having my tablet with me to get all the information that I need. I'll have to check the lists and calculate how much of a load we can put on them. We did bring the generators but fuel will be a concern."

I nod my head in agreement. "Okay, then let's just start with getting all this stuff inside." I turn to the boys. "Matty, Ben, you two start carrying the plants into the atrium and stack them along the far wall for now and us girls will carry in the bins to the kitchen. It's going to take a while to sort through everything that we brought so let's just start with relocating everything indoors."

We get to work moving everything, with some bins being so heavy that two of us are needed to carry them inside, but slowly the pile disappears. Joslin and Sasha stay inside to start sorting the goods while Belle and I head out to grab the last two bins.

I've just bent over to pick up mine when the sound of engines reach us and I stand up again.

Belle and I both turned toward the gates and my hand automatically reaches down to rest on my holstered handgun that's not there. I blow out an annoyed breath. It's been less than a week since the General disarmed me and I've already gotten used to not carrying one around. I never even thought about being un-armed this morning. That's going to need to change. It's a dangerous world out here even if it seems like there's no one around and we're going to have to protect ourselves every minute of every day just in case.

Thankfully, we see Marsh push the gates open to allow the cargo truck, my dad's pickup truck and surprisingly, a tractor pulling a flatbed trailer with what looks like farming attachments on it through. They must have driven down to the planting fields and got it this morning. Clearly they had no problems, but it concerns me that they went somewhere we didn't know they were going and we have no way to communicate with each other if something had gone wrong. We're going to have to have a meeting and lay out some basic rules to make sure all possible eventualities are covered. Right now, I'm just glad they made it back so I stand with Belle and wait for them to drive up.

Lance, Ethan, Jackson, and Rex jump down from the trucks and tractor and head toward us with grins on their faces while Marsh is reclosing and securing the gates. Rex comes over to me and drapes an arm around my shoulder and gives me a squeeze.

"Hello sleepyhead! Sorry I didn't get to talk to you this morning but we wanted to get a jump on things and I felt like you needed a few more hours of sleep."

I give him a smile but motion toward the tractor. "I didn't realize you guys were going to go so far away. I thought you were just going over to the resort. You didn't run into any trouble?"

Lance is the one that answers me. "No, no trouble and that's exactly why we wanted to go right away. We figure it's going to take a while for any of the people we left back there to make it to the fields on foot so we wanted to go and get what we could before they showed up. If they're smart, that's where they're going to head. The only food anywhere around here is sitting down in that field."

I shake my head in disbelief. "You really think they're going to make it that long? It will be months before any of the seeds they planted will produce."

Lance nods his head with a grimace. "It's not just the crops that they're going to be after. There were four pallets of MREs sitting in one of the supply tents they set up. They moved them there for when they were going to relocate the workers to live on site. We took one pallet with us along with the tractor and the attachments that we will need to plant our own crops up here, but Jackson made a good point. He reminded us that not all the soldiers were bad or agreed with his father's plans. Right now, they face starvation so we felt it was the right thing to do to leave three pallets for them. If they're careful they can ration them out to last until some of the crops start producing."

I look over at Jackson but he has his back half turned to us and is staring out into the distance. He must be having an even harder time than I am with all of this. I might have lost AIRIA yesterday but he walked away from his father. No matter how at odds they were, he's probably still concerned about his well-being. Instead of bringing the painful subject up with him, I leave him to his thoughts and turn back to Lance.

"Do you think that's going to be a threat to us? They're not exactly close to here but they're not as far away as I would like."

He shrugs a shoulder. "I'd like to say no but there's no way to tell for sure. There's no reason for any of them to head up in this direction, especially on foot. There are buildings much closer to the planting fields than these ones so I can see them hunkering down close by to the crops and not venturing too far away. Who knows what any of them will do at this point. Some of them might go in the opposite direction and try heading to Banff to see what they can find there. Some might even carry on past the fields and head toward Calgary. It's impossible to know what will happen in the next few months so we just have to concentrate on our area and make sure we take our security seriously."

I nod in agreement and think of all the things that we need to accomplish in the next while and decide we should have a more structured meeting before we all scatter to jump into projects. Marsh has joined us after closing the gates and Sasha and Joslin have come out as well so I figure now's as good a time as any.

"I think we should go take a seat at the picnic tables and have a discussion before we move on to anything else. There's a lot of things we don't know about what happened yesterday and I'm sure we all have questions. We should also draw up some lists and prioritize what needs to be done first."

I glance over at Joslin but she's looking at her feet and won't meet my eyes. She's going to have to provide us with the information we need to know about what happened in the bunker. Lance pulls my attention away from her by agreeing with me.

"You're right Skylar, we do need some answers but more importantly we have to prioritize our to-do lists and figure out who's going to be doing what. As much as I think we're safe here, at least for a while, I think we should have some sort of guard rotation to keep watch. Let's go take a seat and we can start figuring some of the stuff out."

Everyone starts moving toward an area full of picnic tables but Joslin turns and dashes inside the main building. I stand there for a minute and consider going after her. She might be uncomfortable explaining some of her actions but we have a right to know what happened - I have a right to know. I'm about to go to the doors when she pushes back out of them with a tablet in her hand. She looks startled to see me but then looks away and walks past me toward the tables so I turn and follow her.

I send the two little boys back to the playground to enjoy the equipment some more and settle beside Rex at one of the picnic tables. Everyone's looking at me so I just sit up straighter and start us off.

"I think my biggest concern is what the General is going to do next. I can't see him not trying to find us and retaliate against us. Even if it's only to get Jackson back."

I look over at Jackson but he's glaring in the opposite direction at nothing in particular. Joslin isn't saying anything either so I asked him flat out.

"Jackson, what do you think your dad's going to do?"

His head swings my way and what I see in his eyes has me flinching back. "Nothing. He's not going to do anything. He's dead!" With a jerky shake of his head, he spins away, launches off of his seat and takes off.

I'm completely floored by his statement and judging by the looks of the others, so are they. We all turn to Joslin and stare at her expectantly. She keeps her eyes down and lets out a sad sound before gently placing the tablet onto the rough wood boards of the table in front of her.

Chapter Three - Joslin

My chest aches from the pain I know Jackson is feeling. I wish I could have found a different way to handle his father that would have spared him all of this but I spent years trying to find one and always came up empty. With everyone staring at me, I set my tablet on the table and clutch my hands together before telling them our story.

"The day the bombs dropped seven years ago, I was with Jackson on a field trip to his father's military base. When the alarms started going off and the General started the evacuation of his soldiers, Jackson insisted that I be allowed to go with them. Before we left the base I managed to get an email out to my parents to let them know what was happening and where we were going. They connected with Jackson's mother, who knew the location of the bunker, and along with a group of military families belonging to some of the other soldiers, they managed to make it there before the radiation hit. The General made the decision not to allow any of them inside. He even kept their presence outside the door a secret from his troops. The only reason I even knew they were there is because he gave Jackson and

I a yellow level clearance to talk to AIRIA when he was too busy to deal with us." I pause for a minute to swallow the grief that still floats near the surface of my mind. "When our families became desperate to get inside, they used vehicles to try and ram the door and then fuel from them to create an explosion that damaged the seal enough that we were forced to evacuate to the lower levels. The General responded with AIRIA's external defenses. He massacred them all, including my parents and Jackson's mother."

I need a minute to compose myself before I can continue and thankfully no one says anything to interrupt. I clear my throat and tell them the rest. "AIRIA had the recordings of what happened outside the doors in her data banks and I've been waiting for the last seven years for the right time to show everyone the monster that he was. Last night, the timing was right. I had AIRIA play the video of everyone's loved ones being killed on every screen in the barracks. The General's own soldiers killed him. So he won't be coming after us and I doubt any of the soldiers will either. With no working vehicles and only a few weapons between them all, they'll most likely scatter and try to start again somewhere else. They may stick around the bunker for a while because there are the tents set up to give them shelter but without food, they will be forced to move. I'm sure some of them will head toward the fields because they know there's pallets of MREs there but it'll only be some of them. They weren't a big happy family. Some of the abuses they inflict upon each other over the last seven years won't be forgotten and I imagine more than a few of them will take their revenge now that the General is out of the picture."

They all sit in silence digesting my words until Ethan finally breaks it by leaning over across the table and pats my hand.

"I'm sorry you had to go through that Joslin. Most members of the military are honorable but sometimes power can corrupt. The remaining soldiers will have to make their own way now and hopefully we won't run into any of them in the future. My concern is Jackson and how he's handling this. Am I right to assume he was unaware of the circumstances of his mother's death?"

When I just nod my head grimly he frowns.

"This is a lot for a young man like him to take in. Not only has he lost the only family member he has left, he's learned that his mother died by his father's hand. There's going to be a lot of anger, resentment, and sorrow stored up in that boy for a long time to come. We can help him work through a lot of that but I'm most worried about how he may lash out. Do you think Jackson will hold you responsible for his father's death?"

I feel a tear slip down my cheek and quickly brush it away. "I don't know but I can tell you it's my biggest fear."

He nods compassionately and pats my hand again before leaning back and looking to the others. "We're all going to have to try and include Jackson as much as possible and have patience with him. Everyone here has suffered unimaginable loss but we've all had time to deal with it and work our way through it. This is very fresh for Jackson and we need to be there for him."

Rex and Marsh both nod their heads in agreement. Belle leans toward me with a compassionate smile. "Don't worry Joslin, we will help you and him both get through this. We're all in this together."

I smile gratefully at them but then look back down at my hands. There's so much more to our situation then the summary I gave them but now isn't the time to go into it. After all, as much as I appreciate their support, they're strangers to Jackson and me - it's something him and I are going to have to work out together if we have any chance of remaining friends and saving our relationship.

Lance clears his throat and with an understanding glance at me, changes the subject.

"It's good to know that we don't have to worry about the General coming after us so let's put that behind us for now and start making plans for what we're going to do in the coming days." When everyone nods in agreement he continues. "The most important thing we need to do is get an inventory of everything we have, especially food. We need to know just how much we have and how long it will last us."

I pick up my tablet and thumb it awake. "I can help with that. The list that I gave Jackson of supplies to move here accounted for six months worth of food for ten people. With Jackson joining us we have eleven. I have an inventory of everything you brought as long as you stuck to the list."

Rex leans forward. "I don't know about yesterday when Lance took my place but when it was Marsh and me, we loaded everything that was on the list Jackson had."

Lance agrees. "The two loads we brought yesterday finished off everything that was on it."

I sigh in relief. I hadn't had a chance to ask Jackson before everything happened if he had gotten all I wanted. I glance quickly at Skylar before looking back to Lance.

"That's great. All I need to do now is add in everything you guys managed to grab last night from

Skylar's pantry and calculate how much the animals will produce and I can rework the numbers to give you an estimate of just how long we can go with what we have. I think the very first thing we should do is get the fridge and freezers working so that we don't lose any of the perishables you guys managed to bring."

Lance grimaces. "I can get the generator going but the fuel we have won't last long if it is running constantly to keep the fridge and freezers cold. We should look at finding another way to preserve those supplies."

I shake my head. "We won't want to run the generator for that. There should have been solar panels in the first load brought over. Skylar's dad had quite a few in his storage and they were number two on the first list. As long as they were brought we can get them set up. They won't be enough to run everything electrical that we would like but we should have enough power from them to keep the appliances going. Once we have a hard freeze in the freezers we can unplug them overnight and they should stay cold enough not to melt. We'll just have to remember to plug them in again every morning. We should really try and keep the fuel for the generator for other uses."

Marsh pumps his fist in the air. "Yeah, like for video games! Good call on the TV's, Joslin."

I stare at him in confusion. I have no idea what he's talking about.

"What video games?"

His grin is infectious when he says, "I snagged Benny's Xbox on the way out so we can hook it up to the TV's you had on the list and have some digital battles."

There's a slight grin tugging at my lips as I shake my head in amusement. "Um, okay. The TVs were actually on the list so that we can watch tutorials that I downloaded to hard drives. There's a lot of things were going to need to learn how to do so I thought it would be a good idea to bring the knowledge with us."

Marsh nods his head eagerly in agreement and says, "Yes and video games!"

Lance gives him a light smack on the back of the head with a laugh.

"Sure kid, we will put video games on the list - far, far, far down on the list of things to do." Everyone laughs and the tension from earlier dissipates. Lance glances over at the cargo truck and then back to us. "We brought back a bunch of mattresses and bed frames as well as some other pieces of furniture. I think today we should get our accommodations setup after we do the solar panels. We're going to have so much work that we will need to have a good night's rest going forward. Everyone needs to decide if they want their own cabin or if they want to stay in the main building."

Skylar looks over at the playground where Ben and Matty are taking turns racing down the slide. "I don't know about the rest of you but for now I'd like Benny and me to stay in the main building. I'm not ready to be in one of the cabins. That might change in the future but for right now I'd feel better in the big building."

I chew on my lip and glance nervously at her. "If it's okay with you Skylar, I'd like to stay in the big building as well. I don't want to be alone in one of the cabins."

She just shrugs a shoulder and looks away. I don't expect Skylar to automatically accept me but I hope that she'll give me a chance and that at some point, we can become friends.

Belle speaks up next. "Well, I think Sasha and I will take one of the cabins for ourselves. It's been a long time since we've had our own space and I think it'll be nice to have some privacy. As much as I love you boys, I will not miss the smell of dirty socks!"

I look past Belle to Sasha and see that she has a small smile on her face. She's been very quiet and hasn't had much to say since we got here. I know from the video feeds that she and Skylar have a not so great past but last I saw they had moved forward and were starting to get along.

Ethan echoes Belle in his choice. "I think that's a great idea. Lance and I will take our own cabin and you boys can bunk up in your own. I think it's important that Jackson stay with you boys so that he feels included and you can keep an eye on him."

Lance claps his hands. "Good, so today we will focus on getting our accommodations set up, setting up the solar panels and taking inventory of everything that we have. I'd also like to work on getting the water flowing to the main building. We know there's a well here that's still producing so we can see if the solar panels can handle the load of the water pump in the building as well as the appliances. If not, we can start building more of the mini windmills that worked for us in the past. Tomorrow we should work on clearing a garden area with the tractor and getting it tilled up for planting. We're also going to have to harvest some building materials from the resort to create planting beds for inside in the atrium. I took a quick look in the groundskeepers building at the resort when we were over there this morning and saw a stock of bagged soil in there that we can use. It was probably for the many flower beds they have around the resort but with some good compost it'll work just fine for growing vegetables inside and we don't have to worry about it being contaminated. We're also going to need to create animal pens for the cow and chickens. It's going to take us quite a while to get all this done but it'll be worth it in the end. So, I'm going to go to work on getting the solar panels and batteries set up. You guys can get to work on cleaning out our living spaces before we unload the mattresses. Ethan, you should go track down Jackson and see if he's okay. We could really use his help with a lot of this heavy lifting and I think it would do him good to be busy."

Everyone stands up and starts to walk away. I look down at my tablet and put it to sleep. I should be the one to find Jackson but I just don't know what to say to him right now. I know eventually we're going to have to have a conversation but I'm so afraid of losing him as a friend. I hope if he has a few days before we talk, he'll be able to see things clearer and he'll give me a chance to explain. I feel like a coward as I walk toward the main building to start taking inventory and leave my friend alone to deal with what he's going through.

Chapter Four - Skylar

I stand over Benny as he finishes brushing his teeth and spits in the bowl we have in our room for dirty water. Once he's done I run my fingers through his unruly hair and send him on his way. As hard as the last few days have been with the heavy workload, I'm happy. I've never seen Benny as energetic and happy as he's been since we got here. He and Matty are too small to do a lot of the heavy lifting but they have their own list of small chores they do every day to help out around the camp and they're both loving it.

We've gotten a lot accomplished in the four days since we arrived. All of our individual accommodations have been cleaned out and set up so that we all have our own beds. After finding a few gas push mowers, we've cut all the old dead grass within the fence so that hopefully new grass will grow. The tractor and its attachments have been a lifesaver as far as labor goes making quick work of clearing the contaminated topsoil and then tilling and loosening the hard-packed dirt underneath it so we can plant seeds. Seeing just how quickly the tractor accomplished it confirmed that the General used that hard day of backbreaking labor he forced us to do as a ploy in his sick game of dominance. I'm glad he's dead and we never have to worry about him again.

We've been working every day from sun up to sun down and then falling into our beds exhausted so I'm happy to be changing it up today. Lance wants to head over to the resort to scavenge building materials for the indoor planting beds as well as grab the bags of topsoil and pull more car batteries from the many dead cars that fill the resort's parking lot. The batteries aren't really meant to work with the solar system but he thinks he can get them to work even if they won't have a long lifespan.

I'm just happy for a change of scenery so I'm going with him, Lance and Marsh to lend a hand. Ethan is staying back to watch over the smaller boys and he's keeping Jackson with him to help set up a medical room. Jackson has thrown himself into helping us with every project but he's still keeping his distance from the rest of us. Ethan is the only one he seems willing to speak more than a few words with. We've all tried to engage him but he's got his walls full up and most times, he just walks away. I don't expect him to get over his grief in just a few days but having him around acting this way is putting a real strain on the rest of us, especially Joslin. The shadows under her eyes get deeper every day and based on the anguished looks I catch her sending his way, she's going to crack pretty soon. Walking on eggshells around these two is draining so I can't wait to get out of here for a few hours.

I finish strapping on my holster, grab a jacket and head out to the dining area for breakfast. As I pass by the open door to the office Joslin has set up as her room, I catch sight of her sitting on the edge of her bed looking lost and miserable. I carry on past for a few steps and then stop with a surge of annoyance. I turn around and stand in her doorway and take in the room. Blank white walls, a desk shoved into a corner and a double bed against one wall. The room is so plain and empty it might as well be a prison cell. The sad girl sitting on the side of the bed matches that description as well. She's wearing a plain military uniform with no decorations or accessories so it could easily be a prison uniform. My frown deepens and my tone is harsher than I intend it to be.

"Joslin! Grab your gear. You're coming to the resort with us."

She flinches at my tone but then shakes her head. "Uh, I have some calculations and schedules to work on today."

I roll my eyes. "No, you don't. Leave your lists and get your gear. It's field trip time!" I don't give her a chance to reply, just turn and walk away. That girl needs to get out of her own head for a few hours.

I walk into the dining area and see everyone else has beat me here. I take a quick look at Ben's plate to make sure he's eating and then head to the serving counter and dish up a plate of scrambled eggs and a few slices of tomatoes. I'm relieved my laying hens weren't too traumatized by the move and are still producing eggs. I make a mental note to pull out five or six hens and put them into a separate area with the rooster so they can start clutching. It will be good to breed more chicks to expand our flock. With this many people, we'll go through what they're laying every day. Increasing the flock is important to improve our egg production and then we can also start culling the older hens for another source of meat. Ideally, I'd like to triple the number of hens that are laying between now and winter. Even with the supplies we brought, having that extra during winter will keep us more comfortable food wise.

I settle at a table across from Rex and return his welcoming smile. We haven't had much time together one on one but I'm looking forward to spending more time with him once most of our major projects are finished. After a few bites of breakfast, Joslin comes in and nods tentatively at me when I raise my eyebrows at her. I turn down the table to where Lance is sitting.

"Joslin's going to come with us today to help."

He looks over at her in surprise but just nods his head in agreement. I look past him and see Sasha who has an expression of longing on her face. I open my mouth to invite her to come with us, she must be ready for a change of scenery too, but a glance at Belle has me closing my mouth. Belle's expression tells me she doesn't want Sasha going anywhere. She's kept her daughter on a tight leash since our last blow up so I'll leave it to her to decide where Sasha goes and with who. Belle leans forward and looks down the table at the rest of us with a forced smile.

"Sasha and I are going to be busy today as well. We're going to make bread and buns now that Lance has gotten the ovens working." She turns to the younger boys. "Ben, Matty, it's a very big job so we're going to need both of you to help us. Are you up for it?"

Both boys nod in excitement and I try not to laugh. I know they're not excited about the work but about getting first dibs on whatever Belle and Sasha bake.

Ethan does laugh. "Well, I'm looking forward to whatever you produce. Fresh bread sounds great. Jackson and I are going to set up our mini medical clinic today while you're gone. I don't expect any of us to have any injuries but it's best to be prepared just in case."

Lance finishes the last bite on his plate and stands to carry it over to the dirty dish bin. We've all been taking turns on cleanup duty but Belle has been doing most of the cooking since we got here. She seems to really enjoy it so I don't feel guilty leaving the work to her.

Lance leaves his plate in the bin and heads for the door calling over his shoulder. "Okay, finish up and meet me at the truck. We might need to do more than one load so we should get going soon. Make sure you check your weapons before we leave. I doubt we will have any problems but like Ethan said, it's best to be prepared for anything."

I'm just finishing the last of my eggs when Marsh pushes back from the table and gets to his feet. He glances briefly at Rex before looking down at Jackson. "Hey man, why don't you come with us? I'm sure my dad doesn't really need any help setting up his clinic."

I grit my teeth in annoyance. I know Marsh is just trying to help get Jackson more engaged but I'm really looking forward to getting away from the tension and I already caved and invited Joslin to come with us. Jackson doesn't even look up from his plate when he grunts out a "no".

Marsh tries again. "Dude, come on. It'll be fun. There's a lot of cool stuff over there to check out."

Jackson shoves away from the table to his feet and barks back at him, "I said no!", before turning on his heel and stomping out of the room leaving his dirty dish on the table.

I glare at his back as he leaves the room. I get that the guy is in pain but I'm getting really sick of his attitude and how he keeps taking it out on us.

Marsh shakes his head and sighs. "Man, I hope that guy snaps out of it soon."

Ethan frowns toward the door Jackson exited and then turns to Marsh. "We just need to have patience with him. He's going through a lot right now and it's going to take him a while to work his way through it."

Marsh makes a face at that. "I get it Dad but it's still hard to deal with him when he stonewalls us at every turn. We've been trying to get him to talk to us at night in our cabin but he just ignores us and rolls over on his bunk giving us his back. Honestly, he's treating us like we're the enemy and he's our prisoner or something."

Ethan nods. "He's a very angry young man right now. Try not to take it personally. You guys should get going, Lance is waiting for you. I'll talk to Jackson today while you're gone and see if I can get him to loosen up a bit. Be safe out there kids and I'll see you when you get back."

That's all I need to hear to push it from my mind. Let Ethan deal with Jackson, I have some plans for today that don't involve walking on eggshells around anyone. The rest of us take our plates and leave them in the bin for washing and head out to meet Lance at the truck. Joslin follows along behind me like a puppy dog without saying a word. I'm not the only one that's going to benefit from being away from Jackson and all the tension today.

It's a short drive over to the resort from our camp. When Lance drives up to the property I look around eagerly and take my first look at what we have to work with. Rex had told me a little bit about the resort but I'm amazed at just how big it is. It has multiple rows of townhouse-style units surrounding the large central property. I try and picture how it looked before the bombs dropped and killed all the vegetation. I see multiple water features, pathways and flower beds everywhere surrounding the buildings. It would have been so beautiful back then with the mountains as a backdrop. When Lance slowly drives past the main lobby doors I tap his arm.

"You can drop Joslin and me off here."

He slows to a stop and gives me a confused look. "Why here? We've been pulling apart some of the units at the end of that row for building material," he says while pointing further into the parking lot.

I give him a cheeky smile. "Great! We will meet you guys down there once we're done. Joslin and I have some shopping to do in the stores here first."

His expression turns to amusement. "Ah, shopping! Got it." He looks at Joslin quickly and then back to me. "You guys watch your surroundings. I doubt anyone has been here since we were here yesterday but you just don't know so keep aware." He gives us one more look before waving toward the lobby doors. "Have fun ladies!"

Joslin and I jump out of the truck and slam the doors behind us. We stand under the lobby portico watching as the truck drives further into the parking lot toward another building. Once I see it stopped and know where to meet up with them, I turn to Joslin.

"So are you ready to get your shop on?" When she gives a half-hearted shrug, I roll my eyes. "Come on Joslin, this is going to be fun. Rex told me that there's an entire hallway filled with stores that have been barely touched by looters!"

She looks over at the lobby doors hesitantly and then back to me. "Okay, but what are we looking for?"

I study her for a moment and wonder if I should have pushed Belle to let Sasha come with me instead. I'm looking for a little bit of fun here and a depressed Joslin isn't helping with that. I'm here with her now though so I try and get a spark going in her.

"When was the last time you had something that was yours? You know, not from the bunker's inventory but something you picked out just because you liked it?" When she just looks down at her feet sadly, I let out an exasperated sigh. "Joslin, we are going in there and we are picking out some new clothes that WE like. Not clothes that we have to make or anything that looks like a uniform. We will then go and find stupid, totally unnecessary decorations for our rooms and anything else that is fun and pretty and doesn't contribute in any way, shape or form toward our survival. Got it?"

She looks up at me and a small smile starts to form on her lips when she nods. It's not a girly squeal of shopping glee, but I'll take it. I grab her arm and steer her toward the doors.

"All right! Let the shopping montage begin!"

The lobby is filled with early morning sunlight from the large windows letting us clearly see the signs hanging from the ceilings that point us in the direction we need to go. Rex had told me that the hallway of stores was in its own wing and that there was good light from exterior windows but I brought along a couple of flashlights just in case. Excitement builds in me as we come to the entrance to the wing of stores and I stop for a minute and take in the hallway. It's been a very long time since I've been in any kind of store and it brings memories of shopping with my mom flooding back. Shopping was one of the things we loved to do together. We would often spend an entire Saturday just trying on different outfits for fun. I glance over at Joslin who's looking from store to store and hope she'll get into the spirit of this. Even if she doesn't, I have enough excitement for both of us.

The first store in the hallway is a huge gift shop that has shelves of artisan gifts, crafts and racks of clothing with the resort logo on them. Everything from t-shirts, sweaters and winter jackets hang waiting for us to sort through them. Everything has a coating of dust on it but there's no damage to the store that I can see. I'm sure that the guests staying here when the bombs dropped were more concerned with getting back to their homes then looting a gift shop. When I move deeper into the store I do see that the food area where guests would find snacks has been completely emptied out. I step behind the counter and grab a bunch of plastic bags with the resort logo on them and hand half to Joslin. We separate and I start pulling anything that catches my interest off shelves and hangers. My favorite part of this store is the toy section. All kinds of games, stuffed animals, and plastic vehicles go into my bags for the boys. I'm so happy to be able to find these silly things for Ben and Matty to play with. I'm even happier when I find the racks of paperbacks. It's been so long since I've had a paper book that I could read that I don't even bother checking the titles, I just scoop one of each into my bags until the weight of everything that I've grabbed is too much for me.

I look down at the bags surrounding my feet and realize that I've gone a little bit overboard. This is just the first store I plan on hitting but I don't care. Today there is no such thing as overboard. Today is all about unnecessary fun. I drag my bags over to the door where Joslin is waiting and laugh when I see that she's only packed four bags full of stuff. Just before I reach the door I notice a display of posters off to the right and head that way. There's a cardboard container filled with rolled up tubes of posters with a display above it of smaller versions of what's inside. When I see all the different images I start pulling tubes out. Posters of superheroes and huge transforming robots go into my pile as well as a few colorful landscapes that remind me of my mother's paintings. I call it good and drag everything out the door into the main hallway of the wing and leave them in a pile in the center of it.

Joslin adds her four bags to the pile and looks at everything that I have brought out with huge eyes.

"Uh, Skylar? Are you sure you got everything because I think there's a few more things left in that store."

Her expression and tone are so bland that I'm ready to blast her for ruining my fun when I meet her eyes and see that they are dancing with amusement. Hmm, the girl has made a joke. There might be hope for her yet.

I let a grin spread across my face and tilt my head in the direction of the store across the hall.

"Next?"

She sweeps her arm toward it with a nod and says, "Lead the way!"

When we reach the doors to the next shop we both stop and stare. Even dusty, the colors scream out to us after living for so long in a gray world. When we step into the store we're both quiet as we reach out to touch the beautiful fabrics of the high-end clothing this boutique sold. At first we don't even grab any clothing off the racks. We just wind our way through them, reaching out and touching and stroking the fabrics until we get to the back of the store where the wall is lined with shoes, purses, and hats. When we meet back there, we turn and look at each other with something close to reverence before we have that perfect moment of girl glee. The squeal I had imagined finally erupts from Joslin and I find myself bouncing up and down in excitement like the teenage girl I've never been allowed to be. We speed back toward the front of the store and race to the counter to grab slickly laminated thick paper gift bags to fill.

If I had ever had any teenage fantasy shopping spree dreams they would have been fulfilled in that store as I tried on every outfit they had. At one point I looked over and see Joslin wearing a massive brimmed sun hat with a huge bow on the side of it. The giggles that erupt out of me are not a sound that I have made since I was a little girl. So I turn and race to find my own outrageous hat. After I've satisfied my clothing lust I move over to the small men's section and start filling bags with beautiful cable knit sweaters in vibrant greens and blues for the guys. Once I'm done in the men's section I decide that Belle and Sasha deserve some clothing love as well and take the time to stuff multiple bags with things I think they would like.

By the time Joslin and I have stripped a good portion of the inventory of the store, our pile of bags in the hallway has grown out of control. I look down the hallway at more of the shops waiting for us and then back to the mound of bags we've accumulated. Joslin comes up beside me and sighs out happily. She looks down at the bags in the hallway and makes a face.

"Huh, that's a lot of bags. How are we going to move all of that back to the truck?"

I shake my head with a laugh. "I have no idea but I do know that I'm taking every single one of them with us! I guess we should keep an eye out for some kind of service cart or something that we can use to move all of it. This is a hotel so there's bound to be laundry carts around." I shake my head again. "I don't know. We'll figure it out. There's at least one more store in here that I want to go to so let's keep moving."

Joslin's laughter is all I need to start feeling a bond with her so I link my arms through hers as we head to the next door.

Chapter Five - Joslin

With our shopping mania mostly satisfied, we move at a slower pace. The next door that Skylar pulls me through leads to a combination art gallery and home décor boutique. As I wander through the dusty display tables of crystal figurines and embroidered pillows I feel a glow in my chest that I don't ever remember feeling before. It takes me a few minutes to realize it is contentment. I feel happy. There are no lists for me to look at, no video feeds to monitor or plans to keep track of. For the first time in my life, I'm just a girl shopping with a friend with nothing to worry about. Jackson and his misery hover at the back of my mind but I keep it firmly pushed back there and enjoy every second of this experience.

I hadn't really thought about what my life would be like after I got the justice I wanted against the General. I just thought I'd be somewhere else with other people trying to rebuild some kind of life. I never really thought about having friends, or fun, for that matter. I've watched and admired Skylar for so long on a screen and imagined what it might be like to be friends with her in real life. This little shopping excursion had never crossed my mind but it's the perfect experience to start building a friendship with her. I think after this, I should have a conversation with her about what happened to AIRIA. I'm worried our fledgling friendship is too fragile. I don't want to lose what's happening with her by going into the details of how I made AIRIA self-destruct.

When she calls me over to where she is standing at a shelf that was once full of scented candles I push those thoughts to the side. I just want a few more minutes of enjoyment with her.

She holds out a fat pillar candle to me and says, "You have to smell this. It smells like an apple pie!"

I take the candle from her hand and rub off some of the dust before sniffing it. I'm sure before the bombs dropped the candle had a stronger smell but it's faded over the years. I can still smell the scent it's been infused with faintly and I bet once it's lit the smell will be richer. I hand it back to her with a smile.

"That one definitely makes the list. What other scents are there?"

"Well, this section has definitely been looted but there's still plenty left for us to choose from. Let's load up some bags and then move on. I don't know how long it's been but I'm sure the guys are wondering where we are."

I happily go get the bags from behind the counter where a long-dead cash register rests. It's kind of nice to know that there are people out there thinking of me and wondering where I am. Since we arrived at the camp I've been taking it hour by hour and trying not to think about my future there but I'm starting to realize that I could have a real life with these people. So far everyone has been kind to me even though I'm a total stranger to them. I had watched a few of them on the video feeds as Skylar interacted with them and they all seemed like good people. I'm not quite sure about Sasha but so far even she seems to be nice. I'm just grateful that they seem to accept me and include me in their plans for a new community.

Once we filled way too many bags we leave the boutique and add them to the huge mound in the hallway. The last store we go into at the end of the hall is a combination café and convenience store. All the food products are gone but there's still plenty of other items to choose from. Skylar heads over to the convenience area where guests could get drugstore products while I browse through the shelves of the café. I find plenty of travel mugs and vacuum sealed bags of whole coffee beans as well as a variety of fancy flavored teas that I fill the logoed bags with. The next display has expensive coffee presses and hand grinders that I scoop up. I've never been a coffee drinker but I'm sure some of the others would appreciate these finds. I leave my bags at the door and wander over to Skylar to see what she's grabbing. I'm somewhat surprised to see her loading packages of different types of makeup into a bag. She sees my look and shrugs her shoulders.

"Yeah - not really my thing, but Belle and Sasha might want them. Honestly, I don't even know how to use this stuff! Who knows, maybe one day I'll get them to show me how to put this goop onto my face for some reason."

I shrug right back. "I'm with you on that one. I don't even think there was makeup in the bunker's inventories. I guess that stuff just doesn't matter much anymore, but wouldn't it be nice if we could get back to a time when maybe it did?"

Skylar looks down at the compact in her hand and then meets my eyes. "I think we will. No, I believe we will. It'll take time but we will get to a point when living isn't just about going from meal to meal. I believe we're going to make that happen."

I nod in agreement. "I think so too but there's a lot of hard work to do between now and then so we should probably wrap this up and get back to the guys."

She laughs and says in a fake whiny voice, "Aw, do we have to?"

I laugh along with her but then turn serious. "Skylar, I just wanted to tell you how much this means to me. I mean, including me in this little shopping spree. I know there's probably some things we should talk about and some things you're not really happy about that I've done."

She holds up a hand to stop me from saying anything else.

"Joslin, as far as you watching me and Ben all these years, I get that the General made you do that. And even though it rates pretty high on the creepy factor, I have to look at it in a positive light. If you had never watched us and gotten to know us you might not have been willing to help us when we needed it the most - so I think we should just leave that in the past where it belongs and move forward. As for AIRIA, that one still hurts pretty bad but I also understand why you did it. The idea of all those soldiers having control of her makes me shudder. And if I'm honest with myself, I knew at some point I would have to let her go, so you taking that decision out of my hands may have made it easier." She sighs and tilts her head toward me. "I think we've both been through some pretty crappy years. I get the feeling you're a lot like me when it comes to control issues. We're both going to have to learn to let go of things and take it day-by-day. So let's just consider this day a win and keep on going."

I feel tears pressing at the back of my eyes. I can't believe how generous she's being toward me. I know what she's lost in AIRIA shutting down, so for her to let it go and develop a relationship with me is amazing. I bite my lip as I search for the words to tell her how sorry I am again but before I can say anything, we hear voices calling out from the hallway.

Skylar lets out a long sigh and looks at me sadly. "I guess that means shopping time is over." She takes one more look around the store and shrugs her shoulders. "Oh well, there's nothing saying we can't come back!"

I let a smile spread across my face as I nod my head. "You're right, we can come back if we want to. We can do whatever we want."

Her smile matches mine when she turns her head toward the doors leading to the hallway and straightens her shoulders. "All right then. Let's go face the music!"

As we walk toward the doors I have to suppress a giggle that wants to burst free. It's crazy, I'm not a giggle kind of girl. I don't even know if I've ever giggled in my life. When we get into the hallway and walk toward where we've left all of our bags I see Lance, Marsh, and Rex waiting for us. Lance looks up from the pile with an incredulous look on his face while Marsh is bent over double howling with laughter. Rex is just shaking his head with a huge smile across his face.

Lance sputters a few times before finally getting out, "Skylar you can't be serious?"

She just drops the latest bags onto the pile, crosses her arms and lifts her nose in the air and states in a haughty tone, "Fetch a porter for my bags, boys!"

This just sends Marsh into even more convulsions of laughter while Lance pins Skylar with a stern look. I look between him and Skylar nervously wondering if he's going to make us put some of it back but she just stares him down until his expression finally cracks into a smile. He throws his hands into the air.

"And I thought Belle and Sasha were high maintenance!" He gives Marsh a shove and points at the pile. "Come on you lunatic, start porting!"

Rex is smiling when he reaches down and scoops multiple handles of the bags with both hands. He turns and looks at Skylar and asks, "What is all this stuff?"

She keeps her nose in the air when she replies, "Presents! We're having Christmas in… June?" She sends a quick questioning look my way and when I nod my head that yes, it is June, she turns back to him. "June. Santa is coming in June this year."

His eyes sparkle with amusement, "Does that make you her elf, Joslin?"

Skylar throws her arm around my shoulders and grins. "Nope, we're co-Santas! This was a joint effort in shopping mania."

The warm glow I had been feeling expands even more at her words of inclusion and my smile widens even more. Lance just laughs and points to the pile. "All right, let's get this stuff loaded into the truck. We're all done with the building supplies so let's get back to camp. I don't know about you guys but I'm ready for lunch!"

It takes us multiple trips to get it all loaded with lots of laughter and teasing from the guys. I'm riding on a happy high when we pull up in front of the main building back at camp. I jump down from the truck, excited to unpack it all and hand out some of the stuff we got to everyone when Ethan and Jackson come out of the building to lend a hand. I'm in such a great mood that I forget for a second what Jackson is going through and bounce over to him.

"Jacks! Wait till you see what I got for you!"

He pins me with a harsh look of disdain. "I don't want anything from you!" He spits out viciously, causing all the joy I had been feeling to drain out of my body. I literally feel my whole body sag in misery at his ugly words and tone. He shoves past me knocking into my shoulder causing me to stumble to the side. His brutal treatment of me tells me he's never going to forgive me.

Chapter Six - Skylar

It takes me a second to get over the shock of what Jackson has just said and done to Joslin. Rage fills me and any thoughts of being patient with what he's going through fly away as I stomp up to him and get right into his face.

"You're done here! Get your gear and get into the truck. I'm taking you back to town where you can find some of your father's soldiers to live with because clearly, you don't want to be here with us!"

The complete shock and panic on his face at my words has my temper cooling somewhat but not enough to back down. Ethan rushes over and says my name in warning.

"Skylar, don't -." But I cut him off abruptly.

"No! No, Ethan."

I turn back to Jackson.

"Jackson, I know what you're going through but we are not your enemies! You have to stop treating us like we are."

His expression changes to a snarl. "You have no idea what I'm going through!"

I take a step back at the fury in his tone and shake my head and then hold my hands up to him.

"Do you see? Do you see what's on my hands?" At his confused expression I look down at my hands. "They're covered in my mother's blood. I don't even have to imagine it. I can see the blood covering my hands from where I tried to hold it in her body. I can see the blood like it just happened. When I failed to save her."

I don't look back at him, I just stare at my hands lost in the memories that come rushing back and whisper, "My dad's naked body frozen to the ground. These hands weren't strong enough to pull him up. He was frozen solid to the ground so all I could do was go dig up rocks with these hands and carry them back to cover him up."

Jackson sucks back a tortured gasp that jars me out of the memory and I lift my eyes to his. All my anger is gone now. "Every single person here knows what you're going through, Jackson. Because every single person here has had an unimaginable loss. We've all lost people we love."

The fury has left his eyes to be replaced by tears that well up and start to pour down his face.

"I know. I know everybody's lost people. But how do I go on knowing what I come from?" His voice cracks in anguish. "I'm the son of a monster!"

Joslin pushes past me. "No! You're not! You don't come from him. You're not his son!" She reaches out and takes his hands. "Think about it, Jackson. Are you anything like him? Do you want to control all of us or turn us all into slaves? Do you want to be cruel?"

When he gives his head a jerky shake, she goes on. "You're not his son! Never once has he treated you like a son, right? Even before the bombs dropped, you would tell me about how awful he was. How he never showed you love or affection. He wasn't a father, he just donated some DNA. No, you come from your mother. You are your mother's son. No one else's."

His whole body shudders with the pain he's feeling and it's clear in his voice when he asks her, "Why didn't you tell me? How could you keep what he did from me for so long?"

She shakes her head sadly. "Jackson, we were just kids! What could you have done if I had told you? Things in the bunker were already tense, if I had told you, you would have raged at your dad but it wouldn't have changed anything except maybe put us both in danger. Think about what he might have done to us knowing we had information that could threaten his control over everyone? He might have killed us to keep it a secret! I'm sorry but I couldn't take that chance while we were trapped inside with him. Please, say you understand that?"

His head droops in defeat. "I'm so sorry, Jos. Sorry for everything." They just stand there lost in misery until Ethan steps over to them and puts a hand on both of their backs.

"I think you two should head over somewhere more private and have a conversation. There's a lot you probably need to talk through. Jackson, just know that we all want you here with us and none of us hold you accountable for your father's actions."

Jackson looks past Ethan and meets my gaze with apology filled eyes so I give a nod to him that I agree with Ethan's words. Rex steps beside me and takes my hand as we watch them walk over to the swings. Once they're settled there, Ethan pins me with an unhappy look.

"Skylar, that was pretty harsh. We all agreed to give Jackson time to work through his issues!"

I shrug one shoulder. "Maybe, but take it from someone who knows from personal experience. Sometimes you have to be broken before you can start to heal."

With a frown, he glances over at Jackson and Joslin speaking softly together on the swings and turns back to me with a nod. "You might be right. He seems to be opening up at least. But I want to talk to you about what you said to him, about what happened with your parents. Everything you've described are classic symptoms of post-traumatic stress disorder. That's not something to take lightly."

I give him a humorless half laugh. "Trust me, I'm aware of that. AIRIA diagnosed me years ago. I used to have horrible nightmares where I'd wake up screaming and random emotional outbursts. She might have been a computer but one of her main directives was my health so she had me talking about it with her on a regular basis for a long time. Those memories will always be with me but I've learned how to cope with them so they don't control me like they used to. I appreciate you wanting to help me, Ethan but I'm in a good place right now."

He opens his mouth to maybe dispute that based on his expression but Lance steps in and intervenes.

"My husband, always trying to save everyone! Come on, Ethan, Skylar knows we're here for her if she needs to talk about it but if she says she's good then leave her be." Ethan looks from me to Lance and then back again with a sigh.

"All right. Skylar, I trust you'll come to me if any of your symptoms start flaring up?"

I nod reassuringly. "Of course I will."

I close my eyes briefly and let the sad memories slide away before opening them and forcing a smile onto my face. I point my thumb over my shoulder at the truck behind me. "Now, I have many, many, many presents in that truck that won't unload themselves!"

Rex gives my hand a squeeze. "All right, back to elf mode! Where do you want it all?"

The smile he gives me makes my cheeks heat up and I'm lost in his eyes for a moment as the last of my sadness changes to a stomach full of butterflies. We haven't had any real time together since the General and his troops showed up but now that things have stabilized here, I'm hoping Rex and I can explore the feelings that had started to develop between us. His smile grows wider when I don't answer him right away and I swear he's reading my mind when he steps closer to me and starts leaning in like he's going to kiss me.

The moment comes to a screeching halt when Lance clears his throat loudly. "Yeah, we also need to start building those growing beds in the atrium so we should get going on unloading."

My pink cheeks go full red knowing that he and Ethan are staring at us so I take a step back from Rex and look away in embarrassment.

"Umm, yeah, ok, we should get to work." I stutter as I duck around Rex and head to the back of the truck. The butterflies in my stomach settle a little with the distance from him but don't completely go away. I definitely need to find some free time to spend with that guy, preferably without an audience!

I keep my eyes down as we unload bag after bag from the back of the truck and carry them into the atrium building and leave them in the dining area on the long table. Belle and Sasha, their hands coated in flour, come in from the kitchen and move toward the bags with curiosity.

I point a stern finger at them. "Hey, no peeking! It's a surprise and nobody gets to see what we brought until everybody's in here."

Sasha takes another step closer to the table with the most animated expression I've seen on her face since we were getting ready for our party before the General came. I wave her away with a laugh.

"Seriously, you have to wait for everybody else."

She nods her head eagerly and backs away slowly before returning to the kitchen with her mom. I can't help but smile, this is going to be so much fun. I'm so excited to see how happy some of these gifts will make her. Sasha and I have a weird relationship where we seem to constantly end up at odds with each other. I'm hoping that will change and we can just move into being friends. When the final bag has been brought in, they take up two of the long cafeteria-style tables, I start to try and sort out the mess by peeking into bags and sorting them into different piles. It's difficult because we've stuffed so many things into each bag that the only way I'm going to be able to really sort it all is if I start emptying them.

I glance over toward the door when I hear movement in the hallway and see Rex and then Marsh go by, carrying the lumber they had harvested from the resort for the growing beds in the atrium. I stand at the table watching Ethan and Lance carrying another load past the doorway, quickly followed by Jackson. Joslin is right behind him but turns into the dining room and looks at the two tables full of bags. Her eyes are huge as she takes it all in. When she looks up at me, I'm happy to see the sadness that's been haunting them is now mostly gone.

"What are we going to do with all this stuff?"

My smile grows bigger. "We're going to empty all the bags and sort it out for the others to pick out what they want. It's going to be like Christmas without the wrapping paper!"

She nods her head in agreement and starts to smile as well. "All right, sounds like a plan but... We get first dibs, right?"

I let a laugh peal out of me. "Yep, we got dibs. There's so much here that I don't think that's going to be an issue though. Come on, start emptying bags, this is going to take a while."

We each take a table and start dumping the bags out and refolding clothes when necessary. Once they are all emptied, I work down the table sorting clothing from home décor and toys. As much fun as it's going to be to see Belle and Sasha's reaction to some of this stuff, I'm more excited to be able to give Ben and Matty some of the fun things we brought back for them. I move all of the stuff that we got for the boys to a separate table to keep it from getting mixed up with all the more adult gear we brought back. I want them to have a table all to themselves so they can see just how many presents we got for them.

By the time we've emptied and sorted everything out onto the tables, Joslin and I have pared down what we want for ourselves to four bags each. It's mainly new clothing and things to decorate our rooms with as well as a couple of paperback novels. It leaves a huge amount for the others to choose from and I'm ready to start playing Santa. The next time Rex walks by the doorway I call out to him.

"Can you round up the little boys and everyone else and come on in here, please."

He does a quick scan of the two tables piled high with goods and shakes his head with a grin. "Ready to get Christmas morning started?"

When I nod happily he says, "I'm on it!" and then disappears down the hallway. I give him a few minutes to round everybody up and then stick my head into the kitchen where the most amazing smell of freshly baked bread is wafting out.

"Can you ladies join us in the other room please?" Sasha practically throws the tray in her hands down onto the counter in excitement but Belle reaches out and snags her arm with a laugh.

"Sasha, at least wash your hands first! You're covered in flour and dough."

She makes a growling her throat in exasperation but rushes over to the sink where there's a bucket of water and quickly starts cleaning up. I duck back out to the dining area and join Joslin at the head of one of the tables just as the guys start to file in. I'm practically vibrating with excitement and I can't help but bounce on my toes in happiness when Belle and Sasha come into the room and Sasha squeals in girly delight. This is exactly the kind of day I was hoping for and I can't wait to have more of them in the future.

Chapter Seven - Rex

I study Skylar as everyone files into the room. She has a glow about her that I've never seen before. I think it's happiness. She's happy and she's never been more beautiful because of it. I can't wait to spend some time with her one-on-one. Things have been so up-and-down since we met that every time we start exploring our feelings for each other we've had to put them on hold to deal with a crisis. I'm hoping that all the crises are behind us and now we'll be able to actually develop a relationship that's more than just mutual survival. Sasha's girly squeal of glee has me looking away from Skylar for a minute to see my adopted sister staring at the piled up goods with an expression of awe on her face. It's nice to see Sasha happy again. Things have been rough for her ever since we were forced to move into the hotel. Right now she looks more like the girl I spent the last seven years with.

Skylar claps her hands, bringing my attention back to her.

"So, this is take two. We tried to do Thanksgiving in the bunker but that was rudely interrupted. So this is Christmas instead! Joslin and I gathered all kinds of different luxury items just for fun. We still have a lot of work ahead of us on the survival side of things but to celebrate our new home and a new beginning I wanted us to have a mini celebration that has nothing to do with survival. Please go ahead and pick up all the things you would like. Joslin and I have already grabbed the things we want for ourselves so everything here is for you guys."

I look down at Ben and Matty when they groan in disappointment and ask, "What's wrong guys?"

Matty points at the tables with a disgruntled look. "Stupid clothing, candles, and stuff. Nothing that's good!"

I take another look at what's on the tables and see Skylar heading our way. She has a mischievous grin on her face when she reaches us.

"What's the matter boys, isn't there anything here you want?" When they both just cross their arms and shake their heads she laughs, "That's too bad. I thought for sure that table over there would catch your interest."

Both boys lean around her to get a look at the third table she points at and their eyes light up as they race toward it. Skylar makes to follow them but I reach out and take her hand to stop her.

"This was a really nice thing to do Sky. I'm glad you thought of it."

Her cheeks turn pink but she leans closer toward me. "Thanks, things have been so messed up for the last little while that I just wanted a little bit of fun for everyone. Also, the 'office white' walls in my room and my military wardrobe was getting depressing."

I laugh. "Well, I'm looking forward to seeing you in non-military clothes again!"

Her blush deepens even more, but before she can answer, Ben and Matty start yelling at each other. We join them at their table to see why they're arguing. It's the first time I've seen the two of them at odds with each other since they met. I look down at the table and see that they've put the things they want into piles but they're each holding one end of a poster and glaring at each other so I pluck it out from their hands with a frown.

"What's the problem boys? There's plenty of this stuff for both of you."

Ben just crosses his arms and pouts as Matty glares at him and answers me.

"We both want the Transformer posters!"

I try and keep the smile from my face at such normal little boy bickering. It's really nice to see these two kids acting like, well, kids. They've both been through so much in their short lives that it makes my heart glad that they feel safe and secure enough to argue over something as simple as a poster for their rooms. Skylar tries to play peacemaker.

"Why don't you guys take turns having it in your rooms until I can get back over to the resort and grab some more? They had a whole box full of posters there."

Ben looks from Skylar to Matty and then back to his sister. "That's a good idea, Sky, but a better idea is we don't have to take turns and instead we can share it. Why can't Matty and I have our own room?"

Skylar's glow dims slightly at his words as she asks, "You don't want to share a room with me anymore?"

Ben looks away from Skylar to Matty and sees his friend nodding his head eagerly and says, "I want to share a room with Matty. We can have a boy's room. We're big enough!

Matty bounces up and down. "Yeah, we can have a boy's room of our own and we can decorate it with all this stuff!"

I put my arm around Skylar to give her shoulders a squeeze. "That's not a bad idea. We've got Jackson and Marsh and me in the cabin and it's a little tight with Matty in there too. I'd be okay with the boys sharing a room."

Skylar chews on her lip with an expression of uncertainty before slowly nodding her head.

"Okay. I'm not comfortable with Ben being too far from me but I guess we could set up the office between my room and Joslin's as the boy's room. If we could make a doorway in the wall between my room and theirs, I'd be okay with it."

I nod my head and give her a reassuring smile. "I don't see why we couldn't. It's probably just drywall separating the offices."

Skylar turns back to the smaller boys and gives a half-hearted smile. "Okay, looks like we'll be decorating a boy's room for you both to share."

Ben and Matty start jumping around and high-fiving each other in excitement so we leave them to their planning and move over to the other tables. I glance at Skylar and ask, "Are you sure you are okay with this?"

She sighs. "Yeah, I just… I mean, he had his own room in the bunker but everything here is so new and even though I feel safe here I can't help but worry. I guess it's just something I have to accept. Ben's getting older and it makes sense that he's going to want his own space."

I know exactly how she feels so I nod my head. "I feel the same way about Matty. Every day since my mom died he's been the driving force in my life.

In a lot of ways he's like my own child, not just my little brother. I'm grateful for everything that Lance, Ethan, and Belle have done for us but my number one priority has always been Matty's safety. That day that you found us tied to the tree was one of the hardest days I've had since the bombs dropped. Knowing that no matter how hard I had tried, I couldn't protect him made me feel like such a failure. I'm not ready to see him grow up but at the same time, I want him to have all the things that I had when I was his age. I think in a lot of ways letting him spread his wings a little bit is protecting him. This is a good first step to letting him feel a little more independent and confident in himself." I look over at the two boys who are now happily sorting through the toys on the table and sigh. "Let's just call this a controlled experiment as far as them having their own room. We'll start here and see how it goes. Besides, smack dab between you and Joslin? How much trouble can they really get into?"

She nods her head in resignation but looks past me at something so I turn and look. I see Jackson standing in the doorway with an uncertain expression on his face. After the way Skylar blasted him outside in the yard, I can't blame the guy for being slightly nervous so I'm surprised when she's the one to step around me and call out to him.

"Hey, Jackson, come on in and take a look at some of this stuff. Feel free to grab anything you might like for yourself. There's plenty to go around and there's more over at the resort if we want it."

He takes a couple steps into the room toward the tables but then shakes his head and heads over to where we're standing. He looks back and forth between Skylar and I and then lets out a deep breath.

"Listen, I just wanted to say that I'm sorry for the way I was behaving. There are some things that I'm working through but that's no excuse for how I've been acting. I just want you guys to know that I know you're not my enemy and I'm grateful for the way you've taken me in and included me in your plans for a future here."

Skylar reaches out and rests a hand on his arm for a moment before dropping it back to her side. "I totally understand, Jackson. You're not the only one that's guilty of lashing out. I had my own apologizing to do after I let Rex and his people into the bunker." She gives a small laugh. "At least you didn't point a gun at anybody's head!"

His eyes go wide and he looks at me for confirmation so I just give a half shrug and a nod of amusement so he turns back to her. "Now that's a story I think I need to hear!"

Skylar laughs and rolls her eyes. "I'm sure we all have stories we can swap one night around a campfire. The main thing is we all want the same thing, to have a future without having to constantly be worrying about our safety and whether we will have enough food to get through the next week. As long as you're on board with that plan and you're willing to get along with everybody, you'll fit right in with us."

His face turns serious and he nods his head. "That's exactly what I want for both Joslin and myself. It's going to be an adjustment for a while after so many years under my dad's command, surrounded by soldiers but this is exactly what I had hoped for us for the future. So once again, thank you, guys."

Skylar and I watch for a few minutes as he goes over to the tables and starts picking through some of the supplies. I turn to her and ask, "Do you want some help taking some of this stuff back to your room? We can also take a look at that office and see what we have to work with for the boys."

She gives me one of her gorgeous smiles and nods. "Sure, although I only have a few bags and I can handle it myself, let's go take a look at that room and see what we have to do to get it ready for them."

I scoop up the bags she points to and we head out of the dining room and down the hall toward the room her and Ben have been staying in. She stops halfway and pushes open one of the doors off of the hallway, moves into the room and opens the blinds on the single window so that we can get some light in there. It's just a standard four blank wall office with a desk, a chair and a long-dead plant in the corner.

"This will work. It shouldn't be a problem to haul out this office furniture. There's more than enough room in here to put in a set of bunk beds and that way they'll have some floor space if they want to play in here. Once we put up some posters and maybe some shelves for their books, games, and toys it'll be a perfect boy den," I tell her.

She walks over to one of the walls and puts a hand on it. "My room's just on the other side of this. How do you feel about putting a doorway between the two and then maybe locking the hall door? It's not that I don't trust them - but I don't trust them! I can just see them sneaking out at night whenever they feel like it to go exploring."

I let out a laugh. "I think that's probably a good idea. I can honestly say that is something I would have totally done when I was Matty's age. That will cut down a little bit on your privacy though, are you okay with that?"

She shakes her head in disbelief. "Privacy? I've been stuck in a bunker with a little boy for seven years. What's this privacy you speak of?"

I nod slowly with a smile. "I understand that! It's been a long time since I've had my own space too. I'm hoping that we might get some of that here though. I wouldn't mind having a little bit of privacy with you, I mean, if you feel the same?"

Her eyes dance as she steps toward me. "I think I'd like that too. Every time we plan something together some crisis comes up. I really hope we will have an uneventful summer where we can actually spend some time together." She takes another step closer and I catch my breath at her nearness but what she says next has me bursting out in laughter. "But not before you get the boys' room set up!"

As we leave the room and head to hers to drop off the bags, I have a stupid grin pasted across my face. No matter what happens this summer spending time with Skylar will be a priority for me. No matter what it takes!

Chapter Eight - Joslin

I toss the last pulled weed from this row into a bucket and lean back on my heels so I can arch my back to stretch the ache away. I lift my face to the hot sun and close my eyes to just enjoy every moment of the bliss I feel under its rays. After seven years of being a cave dweller, being in the sun every day is intoxicating. The last month and a half here at the camp has changed every part of me for the better. Being a part of this group, this family and working together to build and grow a future has been more than I ever dreamed of having. I no longer have to hide who I am or what I'm thinking about because everyone here has accepted me completely. The first few weeks were a busy rush of getting all our projects and planting completed but once everything was done, everything just slowed down. We do our daily chores and spend the rest of the time enjoying ourselves. I've been slowly getting to know everyone and every day I spend with them confirms that I made the right choice in helping them and joining them here at the camp.

A squeal of laughter has a smile forming on my lips as I slowly open my eyes and turn my head toward the sound. Matty and Ben are playing a game of tag nearby and the sounds of their glee help to fill the hole that I've had in my heart for so many years. I had no idea that a person could fall in love so fast because that's what it is. I love those two little boys so much and I would lay down my life for them. I glance around the yard and see Skylar over in the corner under a large tree and it looks like she's either digging something up or burying something. Lance and Rex are over at the trucks with the engine hoods up doing some kind of maintenance on them. I keep turning my head and spot Sasha sitting under another tree reading a book with a contented expression on her face. It makes me happy to see her so relaxed. I've gotten to spend some time with her and at first, she was jumpy and full of anxiety. Over the last few weeks though, she's calmed down a lot and now her true personality has started to shine through. What surprised me the most about Sasha is her biting sense of humor that is heavy with sarcasm and wit. I haven't had a lot of female friends in my life so it's with cautious delight that I find my place with Sasha and Skylar.

The sound of a cabin door slamming shut has me turning away from Sasha. When I see a stranger coming toward me, I fall back onto my butt in shock and reach for the holstered handgun on my hip. My fingers fumble with the strap even as the guy walking my way lifts a hand in greeting. I don't know how he got past the fences without anyone seeing him. I quickly scan the yard again looking for any other intruders but only see my people. I'm about to scream a warning when Lance lets out a bellow of laughter. I tear my eyes away from the stranger, who is getting closer and closer to me, to turn and look at him. My fear turns to confusion when I see Lance pointing at the stranger with one hand while clutching his belly in laughter with the other. I turn my eyes back to the stranger in total confusion with my gun halfway out of its holster and see the guy rubbing at his close-cropped hair with a bashful grin on his face. It takes me a few more seconds to recognize the stranger as Marsh. His trademark waist-long dreadlocks have been sheared off leaving him almost unrecognizable. Without all that hair in the way, his cheekbones are more prominent and his icy blue eyes dominate his features. When those eyes meet mine, I feel my cheeks flush with heat that has nothing to do with the sun beaming down on me. I look away to push myself off the ground and to try and hide my reaction to his new look. Who knew that under all that hair Marsh was super-hot!

He comes to a stop in front of me and clears his throat. "Hey Joslin, not liking my new look isn't reason to shoot me!" He says in a teasing tone.

My eyes go wide in shock. "Oh, no! I...I'm so sorry! I didn't recognize you. I thought you were an intruder!"

Those killer eyes twinkle in amusement. "Ah, so you DO like the new DO?"

I feel totally flustered by him right now and I start stuttering out a reply but thankfully I'm saved from total embarrassment when Lance and Rex join us.

Lance reaches out and gives his son's head a rub and declares, "My son has been found! I've been searching for this kid for years!"

Marsh rolls his eyes my way at his dad's antics. "My dad the comedian ladies and gentleman. He'll be here all week!"

Rex barks out a laugh but then shakes his head sadly. "I never knew you had such a small head, man. All this time I thought you were bigger than life with that huge mess of dreads. Now it turns out you're just…well…tiny head man!" He lets out an overly dramatic sigh. "You're going to have to turn in your surfboard now."

I have a small grin on my lips at their teasing banter but the way Marsh keeps glancing my way and the reddening of his cheeks make me take pity on him so I throw the poor guy a bone.

"Well, surfboard or not, I really like the new style. It makes you look more grown up, more manly." The minute the words come out of my mouth I feel the heat of a deep blush flow into my face. Did I really just say that? Oh my God, I just said that! It's made even worse by the raised eyebrows Lance and Rex are directing my way and the cocky expression that forms on Marsh's face.

Lance must see my embarrassment because he steps in front of me to give Marsh's head another rubbing, giving me time to get my composure back.

"Seriously son, I like it. It was well past time for you to cut them off but what made today the day for it?" he asks.

Marsh bats his dad's hand away from his head and turns the motion into rubbing at his newly exposed neck with a pout. "Belle wouldn't help me with them anymore. She said my hair had its own ecosystem at this point and now that we have plenty of water and warm weather, they had to go." His pout turns to an outraged scowl. "I swear she was humming with glee when she started cutting!"

The three of us burst out laughing just as Skylar walks up. She's looking at me intently with a calculating expression. She glances toward Marsh and back to me with her mouth open to say something but before words can form she whips her gaze back to Marsh in wide-eyed shock.

"Holy Frack! Marsh, is that you?" At his sheepish nod, a grin splits across her face. She lets out an appreciative whistle and slinks toward him. "Well hello, handsome! Where have you been hiding?"

Marsh's eyes dart toward Rex and back to her as she keeps moving closer to him. He nervously starts stepping backward to keep some distance between them.

His tone is uncertain when he says, "Uh, Sky? Rex is right there!".

She shrugs a shoulder and says, "Rex who?" in a saucy voice, causing him to flinch back before bolting to the side until he's safely behind Lance.

Lance can't keep his laughter contained and doubles over, arms wrapped around his middle. That's all it takes to crack Skylar's act and she lets out her own laugh.

Rex reaches out and pats Marsh on the back. "Don't worry buddy, I'll protect you from her." He looks over at Skylar with a grin. "You're so mean!"

She wipes the laughter tears away from her eyes with a nod. "Yeah, but he's so easy to mess with!"

Lance gets a hold of himself and clears his throat. "All right, you idjits! If comedy hour is over, there's something I wanted to talk to you guys about." Once he has everyone's attention he nods and goes on. "It's almost the end of July now and we've all enjoyed the beautiful weather but I have a gut feeling that it will be cut short sooner than a normal summer. With the number of bombs that dropped and the length of the nuclear winter we just went through, I doubt we will see a full summer yet. So, I want us to start thinking ahead. As the TV show says, "winter is coming!" When he just gets blank stares from all of us, he shakes his head. "Nevermind - pop culture reference. Anyways, winter will be here sooner than we'd like. We've made a good start on our wood pile but we will need a lot more before the first snow flies. Depending on how harsh the weather is, we might not be able to get out to cut more so I want us to be prepared. Everyone will have to relocate to the atrium for the season so we only have to heat the one area but that will still be a big task. I'd like us to have other options for heating it besides just wood."

I nod my head in agreement. "AIRIA forecasted a shorter summer so you're right about that. As far as the generator goes, we won't have enough gas to run it for heat. We've already used up half of what we brought even with the solar panels and mini windmills you guys made taking some of the load. I'm not sure what other options we have except wood burning."

Lance looks around the circle but no one else offers any suggestions so he goes on. "I think we need to go on a scavenging run. Canmore has been picked clean and I don't want to deal with any of the soldiers that stuck around there either so I'm thinking about going east toward Calgary. It was a long time ago but I remember there being RV dealerships on the outskirts of the city that we can look at for propane and other types of indoor, outdoor heaters." He turns to me. "Joslin, did you guys come that way on the way to the bunker?"

I have to think about that for a minute and I glance around the yard to see if Jackson is nearby so we can get his opinion too, but he's still inside working with Ethan. He's been Ethan's shadow since we got here. Jackson's attitude has improved a lot since Skylar told him off but he still tends to stick to himself or with Ethan. He's started apprenticing in the clinic so most of his days are now spent learning everything he can in the medical field. I focus back on Lance to tell him what I can remember of that trip. "I think I know the area you're talking about. Was there also an amusement park near there?"

He nods his head. "Yeah, I seem to recall there was some kind of amusement park on the side of the road just past those RV dealerships."

I chew on my lip trying to remember everything I had seen along the way when we passed that area and remember that it was only a few miles away that we started the controlled burns of the fields.

"Okay, I do remember there were some industrial buildings and RV dealerships near there. We hadn't gone very far past that section when we started burning the fields. I remember being sad because I've never been to an amusement park before."

Lance smiles at me and pats my arm. "That's good, it means that area should still be intact and hopefully we'll be able to find what we need there." He turns and looks to the rest of the group. "Things have been very safe here so far but there's no sense taking any chances with our security so I only want four of us to head out there tomorrow. Who wants to go with me?"

All of our hands go up into the air causing Lance to laugh and shake his head. "All right, Marsh, Skylar and... Joslin? Are you sure you want to head out there with us?"

I nod firmly. "Yes, I've done my training and can handle myself." It will be a good experience for me to go out with them. I can't just hide behind my tablet and stay safe here in the camp, I need to start going out into the world if I'm going to live in it.

He nods with an encouraging smile. "All right then the four of us will head out at first light tomorrow. Rex, I want you, Jackson and Ethan to make sure to do security patrols around the perimeter a few times during the day just to be on the safe side. I don't expect any problems at this point but it's better to always take precautions. Hopefully the four of us will find what we need and be back in time for supper."

After that everyone heads in a different direction and I gather up my bucket of pulled weeds and gloves to put away. When I turn to head to the main building I'm surprised to see Skylar standing in my way with a strange look on her face. She opens her mouth to say something but then closes it and looks away with a conflicted expression. I start getting nervous that she doesn't want me to come along tomorrow even though things have been really good between us since our shop-a-thon, so I try and reassure her that I'm capable.

"I really can handle myself. I had all the same training for firearms and hand-to-hand combat that the soldiers went through in the eastern bunker. I promise I won't put you guys in danger."

She looks back at me in confusion for a moment before shaking her head. "What? Oh, yeah, I'm not worried about that. I'm sure you'll do just fine if we run into any trouble out there. I was just going to ask you...Uh...you know what? Never mind! It's not important." She gives her head a tiny shake and a smile blooms over her face. "So, do you think we should try and get Lance to let us explore that amusement park?"

I let out a peal of laughter but shake my head no. "My first response is frack yes, but reality says that it would be incredibly depressing. I think I would rather just keep a mental image of a place like that filled with happy children laughing and playing with fun music and yummy smells. Seeing it now, broken down and dirty, never to be enjoyed again would be sadder than never seeing it in the first place as it was meant to be."

Skylar frowns and sighs sadly. "You're probably right. That would be depressing. It really sucks that you never got to go to one, though."

I nod but then smirk. "Yeah, but how many kids are left that can say they get to live in the apocalypse amusement park world?"

She snorts in shocked disbelief at my words so I just shrug and ask, "What? Too soon?"

Skylar throws an arm around my shoulder with a laugh as we walk toward the building. "Well, if you can't joke about the end of the world, what can you joke about?"

Chapter Nine - Skylar

I dump my dirty breakfast plate in the wash tub and head to the door but stop and drop a kiss on Ben's head on the way past him.

"You stay out of trouble while I'm gone, mister. Make sure you listen to Belle and Rex and do what they say, okay?"

He wrinkles his nose and sticks out his tongue at me. "I'm not a baby, Sky!"

I ruffle his hair and crouch down beside where he's sitting. "I know you're not, Ben. But just because things have been quiet and safe around here doesn't mean that something can't happen. There's still danger out there and we never know if it will find us so do as I say and lose the attitude about it!" He looks down into his lap with a pout causing me to wish I hadn't used such a snappy tone on him. "Come on, Ben. Don't be like that. You know I just worry about your safety with me leaving the camp."

He looks back up to me and nods his head but there's a shimmer of tears in his eyes. "What about you, Sky? Are you going to be safe out there?"

I pull him against me into a hug and squeeze until he starts to squirm and then let him go.

"I'll be totally safe. I've got Lance, Marsh, and Joslin with me to keep an eye out and we will all be packing heat." I pat my holstered gun with a stern look causing him to grin.

"All right, be safe, Sky. And remember…if you see any zombies, shoot'em in the head!"

I groan and glare at Marsh across the room. A not approved zombie video game had been played last night causing Ben to think they might be out there somewhere.

I roll my eyes at the kid but reassure him anyways. "Got it, in the head! Seriously, be good okay?" At his quick nod of agreement, I plant another kiss on his head. "Love you, kiddo!" And then head out to where Lance has the truck ready to go. Rex is standing there waiting so I flash him a smile while tossing my pack up onto the seat before turning to him.

"So, on your perimeter patrols today, keep an eye out for zombies. Ben's pretty sure a horde will be by any time now to overrun us."

He stuffs back a laugh and tries to look contrite. "I'm sorry, Sky! I should have made Marsh shut it off once I saw the boys watching. I'll talk to them today while you're gone and try and do damage control."

I arch an eyebrow. "Uh-huh, sure, you do that and be prepared for the three AM nightmare wake up because I'm totally making him sleep in your and Marsh's cabin for the next week!"

He finally lets out the laugh he can't contain and says, "Fair enough." Then he puts his hands on my shoulders and pulls me against him, leaning his forehead against mine. "Be safe out there, Skylar. Don't take any chances."

I let my eyelids drift close as his lips touch mine and enjoy the butterflies that fill my stomach and move up into my chest when he deepens the kiss.

The last month-and-a-half in the camp has been wonderful and peaceful but the best part of our time here so far has been Rex and I developing our relationship. This isn't our first kiss and I know it won't be our last. I try and contain the giddiness I feel every time I think of him as my boyfriend, but even though I've been through so much in my life since the bombs dropped, I'm still a teenage girl and he is still my first boyfriend. We pull apart slowly, still looking into each other's eyes when Marsh strolls up to us and whistles.

"Geez, Skylar, if I had of known that was the type of goodbye you'd be giving out I would have volunteered to stay back so I could have had a smooch with you too!"

I turn my head and pin him with a look. "The only thing I'm going to be giving up to you is one to the head, you zombie loving idiot!"

His eyes go wide as he takes a step back and looks on both sides of himself for an escape route while stammering, "Yeah about that... Well, you see...Uh, did you hear that? I think my dad's calling me. Gotta go!" Before taking off around the front of the truck to the other side.

Rex shakes his head with a laugh and yells out, "Coward!" He tilts his head back to me and plants one more soft kiss on my lips just as Joslin walks up to us with a pack on her back. "Don't worry about things here. I'll look after Benny and we'll be waiting for you when you get back."

I smile my gratitude to him and nod before pulling open the passenger side door of the truck and climbing up and sliding over to leave room for Joslin to get in. Marsh gets in the back seat from the other side and Lance climbs in and settles behind the wheel. He gives us all a look to see if we're ready to go and at our nods, he starts the truck and pulls up to the gates where Jackson has rushed over to open them. With a last wave to Jackson he pulls through and we leave the camp for the first time in well over a month. I watch in the side mirror as the gates closed behind us and send a quick prayer up that everything at the camp will be fine while we're gone.

I'm not expecting any trouble between the camp and the highway so I spend the short drive quizzing Lance on what exactly we're looking for. He glances away from the road toward me briefly and then back again before answering.

"Ideally, we will be able to find indoor outdoor heaters at this place that we can use in the atrium this winter. We're going to have to be very careful about venting anything we use so we don't all suffocate from carbon monoxide poisoning, though. I really wish the camp had a furnace in that building that we could work on getting running on some type of fuel but it looks like they just winterized all the pipes at the end of every season and shuttered it for the winter. As much as I'd love to just find a furnace and install it in the place, I don't have the skills to get that done even with all the tutorials that Joslin managed to bring on the hard drives. So basically we're just going to be looking for all the propane we can get our hands on and any heaters that will run on it. Once we have those and a plan, we can start pulling ductwork from the resort to use to vent them as best we can."

I nod my head in agreement and turn and look out the window to enjoy the sight of trees that are not dead, black, and grey. After so many years of winter where everything outside was dead, the sight of brown bark and green leaves still gives me a happy thrill.

Joslin breaks me out of my thoughts with her own idea. "This area had a lot of oil and gas pumps around, right? Even before the bombs, winters in this region could be pretty harsh so all those little workhouses around the pumps would have to have been heated somehow wouldn't they? I saw a bunch of them out in fields on the drive through and none of them looked like they had electrical lines running to them so what would they have used to keep them heated?"

Lance tilts his head to the side in consideration before responding. "You might be right. It might be worth investigating if we can't find what we're looking for at the RV dealerships. It would mean a lot of driving around to find them though and we have to be very careful with how we spend the last of the gas we have."

He starts to slow the truck down and lifts his chin to indicate we should look ahead. "We're almost at the highway, guys, so I want everybody's eyes peeled in every direction for signs of people around. This truck will be a huge magnet to anyone still in the area. I'm going to pull over right before we reach the entrance ramp and walk up to take a look with the binoculars. If it looks clear, we're going to go as fast as we can to get past the exit to the growing fields. If anyone is still around, it will be there. Hopefully, no one will have a working vehicle so by the time they walk to the highway, we'll be long past."

Marsh leans over the back seat. "Want me to come with you, Dad?"

Lance shakes his head as he eases the truck to the side of the road just before the tree line comes to an end. "No, stay put but put the windows down. Skylar, move over behind the wheel. I want us ready to move if there's someone nearby."

I bite my lip in nervousness but do as he says when he jumps down. He looks up at me and gives me a confident nod. "You got this, Sky. Just like we practiced."

I swallow down my nerves and place my hands at two and ten on the steering wheel as he dashes down the road with the binoculars in his hand and one of my father's rifles slung over his back. I drop my eyes to the dashboard in front of me and try and remember all the steps to driving this huge cargo truck. Shortly after we had completed most of our projects at the camp, Lance had decided that everyone except the two small boys needed to learn how to drive. He, Ethan, Jackson, and Belle all had experience behind the wheel but me, Rex, Marsh, Joslin, and Sasha didn't. The lessons that came from that resemble a reality TV show my dad and I used to watch before the bombs dropped called Canada's Worst Driver. By the end of the first day's lesson, I swear all of us had whiplash from all the jerky start and stops we did. After a week of practice, four of us could manage to drive both the cargo truck and my dad's pickup smoothly to the resort and back without too much overcorrecting in the steering or pounding of the brakes. Sasha was deemed a non-driver after just two days of practice when she wouldn't stop squealing and covering her eyes every time she got nervous behind the wheel. I think she was as relieved as everyone else when Lance gave up on her driving lessons.

Marsh's voice right next to my ear has me flinching. "Hey, just remember…those two dips on both sides of the road are called ditches and you don't want to be in them!"

I almost growl at him. "Shut it - or I'll bury you in one of those ditches!"

He chuckles and points past my head down the road. "Here he comes. It must be clear ahead cause he's not running."

I blow out a relieved breath and slide back to the center of the bench seat so Lance can climb back in behind the wheel. I know if I have too, I can drive this thing but I'd rather leave it to the expert until I have more experience under my belt. Lance closes his door and starts the truck with a nod to us.

"We're good to go so far but once we get on the highway we need to be alert, especially around the exit to the growing fields."

As soon as we leave the entrance ramp and merge on to the main highway, Lance speeds up. The one good thing the General did on the way to the bunker was to clear the road of wrecked vehicles so we don't have to worry about running into any crashes blocking our way. As long as no one has gotten cute and blocked the road since then, that is. All of our heads are on a swivel as we scan the road ahead and to the sides for signs of life but it just as empty and barren as the last time we drove through here on the way to our first day of slave labor in the fields. The other difference is the amount of ash we had to drive through last time. We've had a few rainstorms come through in the last month that have washed away a lot so visibility is good - even if the landscape is still mainly a scorched and burnt wasteland in most areas along the road.

We all let out a collective sigh of relief when we speed past the exit to the fields with no sign of anyone nearby other than a few thin smoke trails in the distance. Lance relaxes his white-knuckled grip on the wheel and leans back against his seat.

"Ok, so far so good but that doesn't mean that there's no one out here so we still need to keep an eye out. Those smoke trails are probably cooking fires so it tells us that there are people at the fields. I don't know if they would have heard the engine going by or not but we'll have to be ready on the way back just in case. I figure we have around thirty minutes to where we're heading so everybody can relax a bit but still keep a lookout, please."

As the miles disappear under our tires, my mind goes back to the day that started all of this. The day I traveled this road with my parents. The last day of normal life and the last day I had a mother. I was so confused and scared on that drive. I didn't really understand or believe what my dad had told us about our world ending. Even after AIRIA told Mom and I the number of bombs that dropped and the death toll, the scope of it was just too big for my ten-year-old mind to really grasp. I honestly don't think I really got it until three years after we entered the bunker when I stepped outside for the first time to search for my father's body and saw the snow and ash that the world had become. I can still remember staring down at my dead iPod on that drive and thinking it was the worst that could happen because I wouldn't have my music to listen to. I shake my head at the ridiculousness of that when hours later my mom bled out in front of me.

Joslin nudges me with her elbow so I turn my head her way with a blank expression, still half lost in my memories.

"You okay? You look kind of lost," she asks.

I blink at her a few times while working at putting those images back into the box in my mind where I store them. I have to clear my throat when it comes out in a croak as I try to answer her.

"Yeah, just remembering back to the day this started. My parents and I traveled this way from the city. It was the last time we were together as a family."

She reaches over and takes my hand into hers while Marsh leans forward and rest a hand on my shoulder. They don't say anything, they're just there and it's all I need to close the box of memories away. This is my family now and I will look forward out of the windshield because the future there is bigger and brighter than the past in the rear-view mirror.

Lance breaks the silence when he slows the truck and points ahead and says, "I think this is our exit coming up. Look there."

I turn and look out the passenger window as we slowly pass what was once a place of family fun that I had been to a few times when I was younger. The skeleton of the roller coaster I never had the courage to ride reaches up on the other side of the fence surrounding the amusement park. More memories flash through my mind of better times but I thrust them away as we drive up onto the overpass and the truck comes to a stop. There's no time for memories now because standing in the road in front of us is a group of six people. It's game time.

Chapter Ten - Joslin

I lean forward in my seat to get a better look at the ragged looking people standing in the road. Four of them are wearing the familiar uniforms that I was forced to wear for seven years and the other two are in civilian clothing. They are so dirty and covered in ash that it's impossible to recognize any of them but I think there are four women and two men. Only one of the men is armed with a rifle hanging from its sling on his shoulder. It's pointed down to the pavement but Lance isn't taking any chances.

He barks. "Guns up!"

The three of us in the front seat immediately lift our guns up and point at the group through the windshield and Marsh is hanging out his back window with his weapon trained on them as well. Lance leans toward his window to yell out at them but before he can, they all lift their hands in the air except the guy with the rifle. He shrugs the strap off of his shoulder and lets the sling slide down his arm until the rifle clatters to the road.

Lance glances our way. "Okay, everyone out. Marsh, keep an eye on our backs in case this is a setup and we're getting flanked."

Everyone's doors open and we all slide out with Lance, Skylar and me heading to the front of the truck and Marsh going to the back. The three of us line up in front of the hood, keeping our weapons raised and pointed at the people with their hands up. Now that I can see them better, I recognize two of the women in uniform but none of the others. Before any of us have a chance to speak, one of the women takes a half step forward.

"Frost, is that you?" she asks.

When I only nod but keep my expression blank, she sighs and steps back into line.

"We don't want any trouble. We're just passing through on the way to the city."

Lance steps toward them and places a boot on the rifle and drags it back toward us causing the male soldier to shrug indifferently. "No bullets left anyways." He mutters.

Lance studies each one of them closely before asking, "Is it just the six of you?" When they all nod their heads "yes" he asks, "Any other weapons?"

The woman who recognized me shakes her head. "A couple of us have knives but no guns, if that's what you mean."

Lance relaxes slightly but still keeps his rifle trained on them. "You say you're headed into the city? What can you tell us about what happened after the bunker shut down?"

Before she has a chance to answer, the male soldier practically spits out a reply.

"A lot of people died, thanks to you!"

He's glaring at me with rage-filled eyes and I'm surprised to feel nothing from his words. After years of being terrified by these soldiers, I no longer have any fear of them so I just shrug a shoulder and meet his eyes dead on when I reply.

"Karma's a bitch, isn't it?"

I hear a tiny snort of laughter from Skylar but keep my eyes on the soldier. I can see from his body's stance that he would like nothing more than to attack me but our guns hold him in place. The woman intervenes in a tone that says she's had this conversation with him many times.

"Give it a rest, Tony. It's time to move on." She looks closer at Skylar and then nods. "I've talked to you before, right? You're the girl that lived in the bunker before we got there. You said the General was your uncle, right?"

Skylar nods. "Yup, we rode out to the fields together. You're Megan?"

Megan nods but this time the guy in civilian clothes steps forward and glares at Skylar.

"Yeah, thanks for letting us into your bunker! That sure worked out just peachy for us!" He says sarcastically with an angry scowl on his face.

Skylar laughs. "Right?! It totally sucked having three meals a day and hot showers. Can you believe how I screwed you over by letting you into my home and then inviting a dictator to come in and enslave us all? I totally conned you!"

Lance steps forward with an annoyed shake of his head. "Enough! You two men have nothing I want to hear so take four steps back, get on your knees and keep your mouths shut!"

He motions with his rifle to get them moving but stops when he catches the look of pure hatred being sent our way by the only woman not in a uniform. He points at her. "Yeah, you can join them too."

Lance forces them back down the road and onto their knees with their backs to us before rejoining us. I keep a close watch on the other three women in uniform but they don't seem to care about how we're treating their traveling companions. They just look tired more than anything. Lance calls Marsh to join us so while we wait for him I quickly grab my pack from the truck and bring it out to the road. I pull out two of the four plastic water bottles I had brought with me and hand them over to the women. I don't feel any loyalty to them but I know that they were probably victimized over the years under the General's rule.

Megan sends me a grateful nod and I wait as the three of them drink their fill before asking for information.

"Tell us what happened after the bunker shut down."

Megan looks over her shoulder at the people on their knees and then back to us with a tired sigh.

"Civil War happened. After the bunker doors shut for good there was mass confusion at first. I don't know why, but there was a pile of five or six rifles in the middle of the yard and once people realized that AIRIA was offline and not going to shoot, they all went for the weapons at once. It was like a mosh pit. I mean, a full-on brawl deathmatch! I saw at least six guys get their throats slit. I didn't want any part of it so me and a couple of the girls took off right away and headed down the mountain toward town. We met up with Tony halfway down and figured safety in numbers so we let him come with us. He's a bit of a jerk but he's one of the better ones. He never did anything to stop some of the abuses of the other soldiers against the women but he never took part in it. Once we hit the highway we ran into the other two civilians and they just sort of tagged along with us. I was part of the crew that transferred supplies out to the field so I knew that we had to get to it before the others did if we wanted food. We kept up a pretty good pace and it only took us a few days to reach the fields. We hung out there for three days eating our fill hoping that no one else would show up. We'd been keeping watch on the highway and on the fourth day we saw a huge group of people heading our way. We grabbed what we could and hid in the trees until we could see what the situation was. Turns out some of the General's command and more hard-core followers had rounded up a bunch of the civilians and were force marching them to the fields to work. We stuck around and watched them from the tree line for two days and decided we didn't want any part of it. When we left and headed this way it looked like they had somewhere around twenty people working the fields with six former soldiers guarding them."

Lance curses and looks away while Megan pauses, so I ask my next question.

"Why did you decide to go to the city?"

She shrugs a shoulder. "Somewhere to go? No real reason other than we thought we'd be able to find resources easier there. We know Canmore's been stripped clean and heading west further into the mountains didn't seem like a great plan so that left heading east to Calgary. We detoured around the city on our way here but it looks like most of the infrastructure was still intact. We figured that the majority of the population would have died off with the radiation wave during the first few weeks after the bombs dropped leaving plenty of canned goods for us to scavenge." She shrugs again. "I don't know where else to go, so the city is as good as the next place. We've been moving pretty slow for the past few weeks with long stops when it rains to collect as much water as we can. Honestly, we should have been in the city by now but none of us have much energy to go more than three or four miles a day."

Lance looks over the three women in consideration and then points at the ground. "Grab a seat on the pavement and hold tight. We need to have a conversation in private."

When the women settle onto the blacktop, he motions for the rest of us to join him on the opposite side of the road. He takes another glance back at them and then the other three further down still on their knees before turning back to us with an arched eyebrow. "What do you guys think?"

Marsh and Skylar just shrug so I give my opinion. "That sounds pretty much exactly what I thought would happen so I believe them. What do you want to do about them?"

Lance lifts a hand and rubs at his forehead. "Well, we have a couple of different options here. I don't really want to let them loose so close to where we're about to go scavenging. I don't put it past those three over there to try and come after us to take the truck. So we could load them up in the back in the cargo area and drive them a few miles closer to the city and drop them off. It wouldn't take very long to take them and get back here and it would give us some breathing room if for some reason they were stupid enough to try and come back for the truck. The other option is a little bit more complex. I have no interest in the three down the road but what about the three female soldiers? Joslin, what's your take on inviting them to join us? We have always planned to add to our numbers and from a security standpoint, they would be ideal as they're already trained on weapons. Do you think they would be a good fit for our group?"

I shake my head. "I don't know. I can tell you that none of them probably have any loyalty to the General's male soldiers but I don't know any of them well enough to say whether or not they'd fit in with us. We'd have to talk to them further before making that decision."

He nods his head and looks to Skylar and Marsh who has his back to us and has been covering the area while we talked. "What about you two? Do you guys have any problem with me feeling them out about them joining us?"

Skylar shakes her head. "I'm good with talking to them some more and trying to get a feel for them. We could always blindfold them and drive them back to camp to see how they do for a few days. Kind of like a probationary period."

Lance nods. "Marsh, your thoughts?"

He glances over his shoulder at Lance. "I'm good with whatever you guys decide. It's not like we're going to marry them. If they don't work out or we get a bad vibe we can always drive them back this way and drop them off. Once they're in the camp they wouldn't really know where they were at first anyways if we blindfolded them on the way in. I say we talk to them a bit more and then decide. But whatever we're going to do we should get on it. I don't think we should make this last too much longer. We still have a lot of work to do in the RV dealerships."

Lance looks over his shoulder at the three women and nods. "Agreed. Let's go feel them out on it."

We walk back over to the three sitting women and crouch down in front of them. Lance takes the lead. "So, once you guys get into the city are you going to look for survivors and try and join up with another community? What's your long-term plan?"

Megan looks at her companions before answering. "We don't really have a plan. We're just going to search buildings for supplies and look for a place where we can set up a long-term base that we can stock and hopefully ride out the coming winter. Why do you ask?"

Lance looks at us one more time before answering her. "We've got a pretty good setup going on and we have enough supplies and crops growing to support a few more people through the winter. We could be open to expanding our community for the right people." He tilts his head toward the three others down the road. "I'm saying those three aren't the right type of people but you three might be if you're interested."

For the first time since we encountered them, I see a flicker of life in their eyes. Megan glances between the four of us before responding. "You guys came from the West, right? Does that mean wherever your setup is it's closer to Canmore?"

When Lance hesitates in answering her, she gives a quick shake of her head. "You don't have to tell me where you are set up, I just want to know if it's back in the area we came from."

"It is in that area but it's pretty isolated." Lance answers.

Megan frowns and sighs disappointingly. "It's not a good idea to stick around that area. Those guys at the growing fields, they're the worst of the worst of the General's men. No matter how isolated you are, eventually they're going to find you and you're going to have a war on your hands. We're done with war and we're done with anything to do with the men we were stuck with for the last seven years. I don't even know if we will let Tony stick around. All we want now is to put as much distance between us and them and try to eke out some sort of life. We appreciate you offering us a place with you all but we're not interested in going back anywhere near those guys."

Lance slowly starts to nod his head in understanding. "Fair enough. I can understand why you'd want to get further away from them so here's what we're going to do. Just for our own security, we're going to zip tie all you guys and load you into the back of the cargo truck. We're going to drive you about ten miles closer to the city and drop you off. That gets you closer to your destination and puts some distance between us and your angry friends. Are you good with that?"

The expressions on all three women's faces show relief when they nod their agreement. We all get to our feet and Lance and Marsh head further down the road to where the other three wait and explain to them what's about to happen. I'm slightly surprised when all three of them come along quietly without objecting to being restrained but I guess ten miles in a truck instead of on their tired feet is worth it.

As soon as we have them loaded and the cargo door secured we all jump back into the truck. Lance makes a U-turn and takes the overpass exit back down onto the eastbound lanes of the highway. We're all quiet for the first few miles as we think about what Megan said about the men that we now know are at the growing fields. Even though there's a considerable distance between our camp and theirs, it still makes me nervous knowing that they're that close to us. It's been easy to forget about the dangers they pose to us in the last month-and-a-half of peace at the camp but Megan might be right. If those guys do find us it will be war.

Marsh is the first to break the silence when he leans his arms on the seat back behind us. "Maybe that lady was right. Maybe we should have gone further from Canmore when we settled. No offense Joslin, the camp is great and it did have everything we needed but maybe we should consider a move after we finish harvesting. I don't know about you guys but I don't really want to go up against those soldiers if they find us."

I turn sideways in my seat to make eye contact with him. "No offense taken at all. I did consider Calgary as an option to relocate to. There are actually quite a few locations in the city that would work to start up a community. Calgary had a lot of green space where crops could be grown and there are a lot of buildings to scavenge for anything we might need. The only reason I didn't choose to go there was the initial logistics of it. I knew that when the time came to run we would be limited to what supplies we could take with us. The camp was the only place I could find close enough that allowed me and Jackson to make multiple supply runs without setting off alarm bells. There's no way we would have been able to make multiple trips into Calgary and back without somebody noticing something was off."

Lance joins the discussion. "I think Calgary might be something we should take into consideration for the future. We're going to have to stay at the camp at least until we can harvest everything we're growing but that doesn't mean that it has to be our permanent home. If those soldiers truly are going to be a threat to us we should consider a few different contingency plans. After we finish here today and make it back home, we should sit down with the others and have a meeting about it. Now that we know where they are and what they're doing, that makes me concerned about what's going to happen this winter. Right now we haven't had reason to have many campfires but once the weather turns were going to be running our fires day and night to stay warm. That's going to send up a smoke trail that anybody who's watching will easily be able to find. Yes, I definitely think we should have a meeting with the others and maybe look at relocating once the harvest is in. It would be a lot easier for us to make a move on our own terms rather than be forced out if we have to run from an attack."

We are all silent after that as each one of us contemplates what it would mean to our group if we have to go to battle against those soldiers. It is not too long after that when we come over a rise in the road and I can clearly make out the skyline of Calgary's downtown skyscrapers and tower. Lance slows the truck down until he spots a break in the guardrail where emergency vehicles used to be able to cross the median and pulls to a stop. I look through the windshield and see about twenty feet ahead of us a faded and vandalized sign, welcoming travelers to Calgary. Just past that, I can see two huge ski jumps on the side of a hill with large, expensive looking houses above them on a ridge.

We get the six travelers out of the back of the truck and cut off the zip ties securing them before sending them on their way. Five of them walk away without a second glance back at us but Megan turns and gives us a sad little wave before running ahead to catch up with her companions. As we all get back into the truck, I take another look at the skyline of the city and wonder if all my planning to relocate to the summer camp had been a mistake. Maybe we should have headed here in the first place. But then again, who knows how many survivors make this city their home and if it wouldn't have just been trading one war for another.

Chapter Eleven - Skylar

It only takes us fifteen minutes to get back to the overpass where we ran into the travelers but now I'm impatient to get this over with and get back to the camp. This no longer feels like a fun scavenging run. We always assumed that some of the soldiers would make their way to the growing fields but now having it confirmed and knowing it's some of the worst of the soldiers leaves me feeling sick to my stomach that at any time our camp might be detected and attacked by them. I can't seem to shake the feeling that we've been living on borrowed time this past month and a half. We knew all along that we might have to defend the camp but the encounter with Megan has thrown a switch in me and I can't help but feel an urgency to do something, to prepare more for what might happen. It's amazing how just one short hour ago I was content with the way things were going and had hope for a continued peaceful existence at the camp when now all I want to do is rush back, rip everything that's ripe from the gardens, pack up all our stuff and get out of the area completely.

The tension in the truck tells me I'm not the only one having these thoughts as Lance drives slowly down the street with industrial buildings on either side. He drives past three different RV dealerships and the chain link fenced lots filled with rows of campers surrounding them as we check out the rest of the area. We come to the end of the road and as he turns the truck around to go back, I spot something that might save us a lot of time here. I point to the building that caught my eye.

"Look there! Hearth Custom Fireplace Designs. Maybe they've got what we need?"

Lance applies the brakes and leans closer to the windshield to get a better look at the sign on the plain industrial building before leaning back with a small smile.

"Good eyes, Skylar. That might be even better than propane heaters. It makes sense that they'd be out here on the outskirts too. They probably have a forge in there somewhere for the metal work and the yard would give them the space they needed for the natural stone for the hearts. If these guys stocked pellet stoves then it's our lucky day!"

He drives up into the parking lot and pulls in sideways in front of the doors before putting the truck in park.

"All right, two of us go in and clear the building and two of us stay out here as lookouts. If they have what we need, I will drive the truck around to the back and hopefully they'll have a loading dock we can use. Everybody stay on alert. There's no sense letting your guard down now."

Marsh and I volunteer to stay outside to keep a lookout while Lance and Joslin head inside after prying the front doors open with a crowbar. We take a few minutes to scan the area and when we find nothing moving we lean against the side of the truck facing the road. Marsh keeps sending me looks from the corner of his eyes until I finally get tired of his hedging and ask him, "What? If you have something to say, just say it!"

He scuffs the toe of his boot against the pavement a few times in hesitation. This is so weird! I've never seen Marsh this way before. Usually he's pretty blunt and willing to say the craziest things to get a reaction. Whatever it is that he wants to say to me must be important to him. He finally lets out a deep breath and turns to me.

"So… um… Has Joslin, like, ever said anything to you… About me?"

I have to bite back my first reaction which is to bend over belly laughing. This is so teenage drama that it's hard to contain. But then I remember how I felt when I first met Rex and how idiotic I felt over my crazy feelings for him. So instead I keep my smile small and feel him out a bit more about this.

"What about Sasha? I thought you had a thing for her."

He rolls his eyes at me and then looks away with the shake of his head. "I kind of came to the conclusion that Sasha's always going to be my little sister. And in case you haven't noticed, since you and Rex have kind of cemented the couple thing, she's turned her puppy dog eyes on Jackson."

I make a, "hmm" noise in the back of my throat before replying. "I see, so you're just going to move on to the next available girl, is that it?"

His head swings back my way with an outraged expression. "What? No! That's not how it is at all. I really like Joslin. She's so smart and cool, not to mention how pretty she is. I swear when she hits me with those cool gray eyes I just freeze in place. Even if there were ten other available girls around I'd still be interested in her!"

I hold up my hand in a stop gesture. "Okay Romeo, cool your jets. I was just checking! I really like Joslin too and I just wanted to make sure that you liked her for the right reasons. As for her mentioning you, no, she hasn't said anything really but I have caught her looking at you a few times with a bit of sparkle in her eyes. I'll tell you what, because I never got to have a normal teenage social life, I'll play high school drama for you. Once we get back to camp, I'll feel her out on what she thinks of you. Once I have some answers, I'll write it down in a note and I'll pass it to you discreetly during study hall. Most likely they'll be a box or two for you to check asking if you want to go out with her!"

The glare he sends my way at my teasing breaks through my restraint and I end up bending over and getting that deep belly laugh I held back earlier. He's saved from saying anything else when Lance pops his head out of the doors and calls our names.

"Hey you two, come on in here and help Joslin pack up some of this stuff. We found everything we need so I'm going to drive the truck around to the back to load it all."

Marsh gives me one more unimpressed look before stomping away past his dad into the building. Lance has a confused expression on his face when he turns to me.

"What was that all about?"

I shrug my shoulders and roll my eyes. "Who knows? Teenage boys are weird!"

I can't help but giggle at his completely baffled look as I sail past him into the store. I find Marsh and Joslin back in a storage room where they're muscling a weird-looking stove onto a dolly. Joslin points at three more similar looking models and uses the back of her hand to wipe sweat from her forehead.

"Lance wants us to take four of these as well as all those bags of pellets over there. There's another couple of dollies just down the hallway if you want to bring them in and start stacking the bags. He also wants us to grab any ducting or pipework they have here to go with these." She looks around the dim room with a pleased smile. "These are such a great find! The brochure for these bad boys says that each one of these forty pound bags of pellets will burn for 24 hours and that the fire is almost smokeless. There's a bunch of pallets of these bags in the back area of the store but we're going to have to try and find more if we can. Lance says that he thinks most of the big box home improvement stores carry them so we'll probably have to make another scavenging run but this time we'll have to go into the city for it. Keep your eyes open for a phone book and grab it if you see one. Sadly I can't google the closest locations to us," she says with a laugh.

We get to work loading up all the bags that the store contains. Joslin and I work on the bags while Marsh and Lance focus on the heavier stoves. We're all tired and sweaty not to mention hungry by the time we get the last of it loaded into the back of the cargo truck so we take a break to hydrate and eat a quick lunch.

Lance drains the last of his water and stuffs the bottle back into his pack to be refilled once we're back at the camp and then looks at us.

"So even though we found what I think we'll need for heating, I'd like to do a run through of the RV places as well. I'd like to grab all the propane bottles that we can find as well as any camp stoves they have there. We're already here so it makes sense to get everything we can. You can never go wrong with having backups for your backups!"

I take the last bite of my cheese and tomato sandwich that Belle had packed for us for lunch and amuse myself by watching Marsh trying to covertly steal glances at an oblivious Joslin. I was only teasing him when I said that I had seen her sending him secret glances so I'm a little bit surprised when it actually happens. When Marsh leans over to close his pack, Joslin takes the opportunity to look at him. Her eyes might not be full of stars and little hearts but there's definitely interest in her gaze. I laugh to myself as I head over and climb into the truck. The way things are going we can have ourselves a regular TV teen drama on our hands. Rex and I could be the reliable couple that stays together through thick and thin. Marsh and Joslin could be the couple that never has the courage to declare their feelings for each other even though the viewers know they're meant to be. And knowing Sasha, her and Jackson could be the couple that breaks up and makes up on every episode. I have a silly grin plastered across my face when Joslin climbs in beside me.

She gives me a look and a small smile in return and asks, "What? What's so funny?"

I shake my head innocently and say in an announcer's voice, "These are the days of our lives… Teen Edition!"

At her completely confused expression I just give up and laugh out loud. Lance gets in beside me behind the wheel and looks from me to Joslin and then shakes his head.

"Uh, Skylar, are you feeling all right?"

I laugh even more at that and just motion for him to get going. Although I still have concerns about the General's men being in our area, it's nice to just be happy for a little while, even if it is over something as silly as teenage romance.

We make quick work of scavenging the RV centers with Lance and Marsh focusing on hauling out as many propane bottles as they can find. Joslin and I focus on the accessories in the parts stores attached to the dealerships. We grab huge amounts of RV toilet paper as well as tarps, tie downs and even some fishing gear that was on display. The best find by far though comes at the second RV location. They have an entire display set up with cast iron cookware to be used over an open fire and alongside that are two racks of dehydrated campfire meals. There is everything from cornbread with jalapenos to beef stew with dumplings. I'm completely shocked that not one item seems to have been taken from those racks when there was enough food on them to last a person a good month. It probably won't go more than a week with the number of people we have, but it's still a real bonus of a find.

Once we have scavenged all three locations, we load back up into our now mostly full cargo truck and head back to the highway toward the camp. For the first part of the drive everyone is in a good mood from the successful day of scavenging but the closer we get to the exit to the growing fields the tenser the mood in the truck gets. I think we all hold our breath when the sign for the exit comes into view until we were a good two miles past the area. I don't know what I was expecting to happen, maybe a bunch of soldiers shooting at us, but nothing did. We didn't hear gunfire and we didn't see anyone anywhere near the road. By the time we reach our exit to the camp I find myself exhausted from all the different emotions that I have run through today and I'm ready to spend some time just relaxing and having fun with either Ben or Rex.

When we pull up to the gates, it takes a few minutes but Jackson appears up on the guard platform we built by the gate and gives us a thumbs up before disappearing again to climb down and open them for us. The first thing I see when we pull through is Rex stationed behind Ben and Matty at the swing set where he's alternating pushing them. All the tension of the day flows out of my body at seeing the people I love the most, safe and sound. That thought makes me pause for a moment. As I stare at a smiling Rex who's started walking our way, I realize that not all of what's going around is teen drama after all. It's love. Holy Frack! I'm in love with Rex! The craziest part about that is…I'm totally okay with it.

Chapter Twelve - Rex

Skylar seems different since she got back yesterday. When she looks at me now it's almost like her gaze has more depth to it. Whatever it is, I like it. It makes me want to be with her even more than I did before. She's the last thing I think about when I close my eyes at night and the first thing I think about when I open them in the morning. I'm not really sure what that means for a relationship but I know I want more of it.

I'm leaning up against the wall in the dining room, waiting for everybody to come in so we can get our meeting started. Lance said he wanted to talk to us all about some contingency plans and what we're going to do in the future. I'm not sure what that means because as far as I know, things have been going really well here and we're on track to have a decent harvest in the next month but I'm open to anything as long as we're all together. I push off from the wall when Skylar comes through the door of the kitchen drying her hands with a towel. Joslin's on her heels doing the same thing. It was their turn on clean-up crew so they've spent the last half an hour washing dishes and scrubbing pots. When her eyes lift and meet mine across the room, her footsteps falter for a moment and then quicken as a beautiful smile spreads across her face. This is crazy, we just saw each other over breakfast so how can I feel like I missed her. I stop thinking about my feelings when she reaches me and leans against my chest and just let myself feel my feelings instead. She leans back from me, grabs my hand and leads me over to the table where Joslin has settled. We sit down just as everyone else comes into the room and joins us.

Lance has his serious face on as he takes his place at the end of the table with Ethan beside him. Marsh, Sasha, Belle, and Jackson quickly join us and take seats at the table. We all turn to stare at Lance expectantly and wait for him to begin. When he sees that he has our attention he starts the meeting.

"Yesterday was a success. We found exactly what we need for an alternate heat source for this coming winter but we will have to make at least one more scavenging run to get extra pellets for the stoves that we found. We won't be able to find what we need around here anywhere so we will have to go into the city to find them. That presents us with a bit of an opportunity. Before I get to that, I want to share the information we received from some of the people we ran into yesterday."

"One of the soldiers was pretty forthcoming with what happened after AIRIA shut the bunker down.

It was pretty much exactly what we expected to happen but now it's been confirmed that some of the more dangerous soldiers are at the growing field, and apparently, they've conscripted a bunch of the people the General was going to use as his labor force. I'd like to say we could go and free those people, but honestly, I'd rather stay out of that fight. I know some of us feel slightly responsible for their fate but the honest truth is that we're not. Skylar was gracious enough to let those people into the bunker to start with but they're not our responsibility and I don't want it to become our fight. So that being said, my concerns are that those soldiers and people are fairly close to us and may pose a threat if they discover us here. So far we've been very, very, lucky that we've managed to stay off their radar but if for any reason they should come this way, we might be facing an attack from them. That brings me back to the possible opportunity I mentioned. We may want to consider relocating completely."

Sasha is the first to respond. "What!? No, no we're safe here, this is our home. I don't want to go back out there. Nothing good has happened to any of us out there!"

Belle puts an arm around her daughter and pulls her closer, trying to calm her, before she turns her head to ask Lance a question.

"Do you really think that's necessary? This is a very good location for us. We have everything we need here and we've been perfectly safe since we got here. If we move now, we will have lost all the work we put into making this place sustainable and we will be going somewhere that we have no idea what the dynamics are. We could be walking into a totally different set of problems!" Her voice increases in volume until her last sentence is almost panicked.

Lance holds up his hands. "Whoa, this is just a conversation about an option we could consider and we wouldn't be going anywhere until after the harvest is in. What I'd like to propose is that when we go into the city to find more pellets for the stoves, we do a little recon of the area. Look for signs of other survivors and see what is still intact. Joslin said that she did consider Calgary when she was looking for a place for us and that there were quite a few locations that would work well. The only reason she picked the camp was because of how close it was. Its proximity to the bunker allowed her to get more supplies here under the radar. That's not something we have to worry about so much now with the General gone. I'm proposing we look around while we're in the city and see if it would be a good fit for us. If we like what we see, then once the harvest is in, we could pack everything up in the two trucks and the trailer and try and make it in one trip.

Worst case scenario is we'd have to make two trips to move everything we'd want to take with us."

I can tell by Belle's expression that she still not convinced. She shakes her head at Lance with a frown.

"I just don't understand why you want to uproot us again. Things are good here. We have a solid plan to make it through the winter. I'm just saying, every time we've moved something bad has happened. The hotel was a disaster from the start and then even though the bunker had luxuries to enjoy it ended up almost costing us our freedom."

Ethan reaches over and lays a hand on one of Belle's. "I understand your concerns, and yes, we have had a bit of bad luck but one of the most important rules we relied on since this all started was one is none and two is one. You know this. Right now we have one home. It's a great home and I love it here as well. What Lance is saying is that if we are attacked or something happens to force us out of here, we'd be running blind. All he's suggesting right now is for us to look at some contingency plans in case something goes wrong. If what we find in the city looks better than what we have here then we might want to consider relocating ahead of a possible emergency."

Skylar's fidgeting beside me in her seat and she keeps sending looks Joslin's way like she wants her to say something but Joslin's eyes are firmly fixed on Lance, Ethan, and Belle and she's missing whatever Skylar's trying to communicate to her. I give her a discrete nudge and arch my eyebrows questioningly but she gives a tiny sharp shake of her head, dismissing me.

Joslin joins the discussion with her opinion. "I think Lance is right. I pushed the drones as far as I could when no one was monitoring me and got a good look at the southwest end of the city. As far as I could tell there was no one occupying that area and most of the buildings and infrastructure were intact. There are a lot of green spaces available to grow crops and lots of buildings to choose from with windows that we could use as greenhouses. If the majority of the population in the city died off within the first few weeks from the radiation there's a good chance that there's a lot of supplies still available to us there. Not just canned goods but building materials, more solar panels and even generators. I'll have to look into some of the information that I downloaded but there's a possibility that with the right additives we could get some of the gas from underground tanks at gas stations to work for us. We also have many more options for fallback positions then we do here. Right now if anything happened, the only thing we could do is run into the forest or if we're lucky, drive away. If we were in the city we could have secondary locations set up ahead of time and stocked so that we'd always have somewhere to go."

When it's clear Joslin's got nothing more to share, Skylar almost seems to deflate beside me. I'm not sure what's going on with her or what she wants to hear from Joslin but now isn't the time to get into it so I keep quiet.

Lance looks around at all of us and asks, "Does anybody else have an opinion on this or something they want to say?" When all he gets in return is head shakes and shrugs he nods his head and stands. "All right then. Let's plan a week from now to head into the city to look for more wood pellets and while we're there, we'll take a hard look at the possibilities. Right now I'm going to get to work on trying to install the pipework to vent the stoves that we brought back, so anybody willing to lend a hand meet me in the atrium in five."

As everyone gets up and files out, I hold Skylar back beside me at the table. We watch as Belle leads an emotional Sasha into the kitchen. I get that she's upset and I understand why she wouldn't want to leave here but she's going to have to toughen up a little bit to survive out here with us. She can't always react with such extreme emotions every time hard decisions have to be made. Once everyone's left the room, I slide away from Skylar a little bit so that I can turn to face her.

"What was that all about? With Joslin?"

Her expression goes blank and then turns to fake confusion. "I don't know what you mean," she says innocently.

I smile because she's so easy for me to read now and I know she's lying. "Sky, you clearly wanted Joslin to say something different than what she did so what was it?"

She shakes her head slowly. "Oh that. I just thought she was going to have a different opinion. But you know, she's the smart one with all the planning and the research so if she thinks that we should look at relocating to Calgary I'm on board." She leans in and brushes her lips against mine before pushing up from her chair. "Well I'm off, I need to take a look at my hens and make sure all the new mommies and the babies are happy. Can you check on the boys on your way to the atrium and make sure they're actually doing some of the school work I set up for them please?"

I give her a knowing grin and nod my head. "Sure, I'll go crack the whip before I go play with the pipes."

She gives me a small laugh and a wave then disappears out the door. I sit there and stare at the empty entrance thinking about what just happened. I know she didn't tell me the whole story about what's going on with her and Joslin but I've learned not to push Skylar. When she's ready to tell me what's on her mind, she will. I push away from the table and head to the boys' room to check on them but all I really have on my mind is Skylar's gorgeous blue eyes and when I'll get to look into them again.

It takes us five long hot sweaty days to complete all the pipe and ductwork we need to connect the four pellet stoves Lance and the others brought back. Our biggest concern is making sure that there is proper ventilation to the outside so that we all don't die from carbon monoxide poisoning. This required cutting holes in strategic places around the exterior of the atrium room to feed the ducts to the outside to vent and then sealing the gaps around the holes we made back up again to keep the cold weather out.

I'm enjoying my first morning off since we started the heating project by spending it with Skylar. Belle is working with Ben and Matty on their math skills, leaving us a few hours to spend together in peace. We brought a blanket out and laid it on the new grass under one of the trees. Skylar's laying on her back looking up through the leaves and branches of the tree while I lay beside her on my side with one hand propping up my head so I can stare down at her pretty face.

"So do you think she likes him too?" I ask.

A small smile curves her lips. "At first I was just teasing him about that but then I caught Joslin giving him the googly eyes so I guess there is something there after all."

I give my head a small shake. "I just don't see it. I mean, it'd be like an owl dating a dolphin!"

Skylar giggles. "Explain that!"

I tug at one of her curls. "You know, Joslin's so smart and serious. She's always watching everything around her and I swear she's got a computer in her brain where she takes notes on everything she sees. Then you've got Marsh who is so laid-back and goofy most of the time that I just don't see them fitting together."

She bats my hand away playfully from her hair. "I disagree. You're just looking at the surface of their personalities. Take Joslin – yes, she comes off serious and oh so smart but there's more to her than that. She has a sense of humor that will surprise you and in the right setting and circumstances, she would totally loosen up. I think Marsh's goofiness would be great for her. As for Marsh, he has a steel core of strength inside of him that you only see when the chips are down. Here's an example, when you and Sasha were prisoners at the hotel, I saw a totally different side to him. He and Lance went into the wing of the hotel to set it on fire to create a diversion and ended up getting into a fight with some of the people in there. When they got back, I swear half his forehead was hanging down over his eyes from being sliced with a knife. I was ready to puke just looking at it but he was all like, "Slap some tape on it we have work to do!" And that's exactly what Ethan did, he just taped it up and off we went to free you guys! Seriously, there's way more depth to Marsh then just his surfer boy persona that he displays to everyone."

"Hmm, that's pretty insightful, Skylar. Who else do you have insight on?"

She laughs. "All right but I'm not trying to be mean or anything. It's just my take on people, okay?"

I nod my head reassuringly at her. "Don't worry Sky, this is just between us. I'm just curious what you think of everyone."

She chews on her lip nervously and scans the yard to make sure no one's nearby before she starts.

"Okay, take Sasha for instance. She's like a freshly baked chocolate chip cookie. Kind of firm on the outside and really sweet but inside she's a hot gooey mess. What I mean is - she's sweet and keeps it together as long as everything is going along fine but the minute things get hard or something happens to change the dynamic, she just dissolves into this mess of panic and sometimes selfishness. I honestly don't know if she's ever going to change. I mean, after everything you guys have been through, you'd think that she would have toughened up a little bit but it doesn't seem like she has so…"

I nod my head in agreement. "Yeah, I know. I get what you're saying and I do tend to agree with that. She's just missing that little bit of steel inside that we all seem to have to get through tough times. We're just going to have to take care of her as best we can. Okay, who's next?"

"Well, Ethan and Belle are easy. They're clearly the mom and dad of the group. I don't know what else to say besides that. Lance is our warrior and chief. He's always going to be trying to protect everyone and keep us all on track with a little bit of dad thrown in there too." She laughs and then taps her lips in thought before continuing. "So that just leaves Jackson. He's tougher to read. Mainly because I don't know him that well but I do know he has serious daddy issues and I don't know if he's ever going to overcome them. He could go either way. He can spend his life overcompensating for all the things his father did or he can spend his life being dark and broody and never quite letting it go. It's hard to say, only time will tell on that one. And then there's the boys who are just, well, perfect in every way!"

I grin down at her. "I think you forgot someone," I say in a teasing sing-song voice. When she just arches her eyebrows at me I say, "Me! You forgot me!"

She sighs and shakes her head sadly like I'm a lost cause but her smile pushes through. "Yeah, what to say about you? Well I only have one thing to say about you Rex, and that is, you're mine." As she says the last word she reaches up and pulls me down toward her until our lips meet and I lose myself in being hers.

Chapter Thirteen - Joslin

I step out of the cabin that we are using as our hen house and once more count the chickens and baby chicks in the section of yard that we've enclosed with wire. The number I come up with is still wrong. Shaking my head, I walk out of the gate and head around to the back of the cabin to look for the missing birds. I come up empty when I make it back to the front and stand there looking out over the yard, trying to figure out where the heck these birds have gotten to. They have to be around here somewhere. It's not like they could fly away.

"Whatcha doing?" Comes from behind me, causing me to flinch and spin around quickly in surprise. Marsh is standing there with his goofy smile and I feel my cheeks heating up. I curse my reaction. I don't know what's going on the last few days with me but I've been jumpy and edgy. It's like a dark cloud of nerves is hanging over my head and I don't know why. All I can figure is I'm worried about what we will find in the city on our upcoming trip to scout it.

Marsh cocks his head at me. "Sorry, I didn't mean to startle you. You look like you were in deep thought or deep confusion. What's on your mind?"

I scan around the hen yard and cabin one more time before throwing up my hands with a growl of frustration before answering him. "I can't find all the chickens!"

His eyebrows go up and he gets a look of amusement on his face before turning and looking behind him at the yard and then back to me with a smile.

"So… is this a game of chicken hide-and-seek then?"

I shoot him an annoyed glance and shake my head. "I'm serious! I've done the count twice now and we're missing three of our hens and three of the baby chicks. I've no idea where they've gotten to."

His grin dims slightly but his eyes are still full of amusement. "Okay, I'll help you look for them. I'm sure they're around here somewhere. It's not like they could have flown away, right? Let's check the wire fence and see if there are any gaps that they might have been able to squeeze through first. If they managed to get through, they could be anywhere in the yard by now."

I nod my head in agreement and we make our way slowly around the wire fenceline, looking for gaps big enough that would have allowed the chickens to get out, but don't find anything. Marsh goes into the cabin to look for any holes or hiding places they might be in while I walk around the cabin for the third time. This is getting frustrating. Where in the heck could these birds have gone to? He meets me back out front with a shake of his head.

"I got right down on the floor inside looking for loose boards but I couldn't find anything. Why don't we walk around the yard and see if they are out here somewhere?"

I shake my head in frustration but wave him ahead to lead the way. We start walking along the wooden fence that encloses the camp, scanning the ground ahead of us for any sign of these stupid birds.

Marsh keeps glancing over at me like he wants to say something, but he doesn't, so after a few minutes of this I finally come to a stop and turn and face him.

"What?" I ask, in amused exasperation.

He looks at me and then looks away again. It's sort of funny because this is the first time I've ever seen Marsh nervous about something. He finally takes a deep breath and looks straight at me.

"So… I was just wondering… Um… If you would want to watch a movie tonight?"

I shrug my shoulders and start walking again at such a mundane question, waiting until he catches up to me to answer.

"Sure. I mean, I don't see why we couldn't watch one tonight. It's been a few days and we still have plenty of battery charge on the laptops so we don't have to use the generator and waste gas. Whatever everybody wants to do, I'm fine with."

He lets out a deep breath that almost seems disappointed. "Actually, I meant with me or just me, I mean."

I stop again and turn to him - totally confused. "You want to watch a movie by yourself?"

Now it's his turn to let out a growl of frustration. "No! I mean, you and I watch a movie…together…alone. Jeez Joslin, you sure don't make this easy!" At my baffled expression, he looks away.

"I'm trying to ask you out on a date. It's not like I can say, hey let's go to the movie theater together anymore or even let's go to the mall. Dating activities are sort of slim on the ground these days so I'm trying to work with what we have."

I feel like a total idiot and at the same time feel a warm flush seep into my stomach. A small smile tugs at my lips. Now that I know what he's doing, I can't help but see how cute he is in his fumbling attempt to ask me on a date. His whole face is red in embarrassment so I take pity on him.

"Marsh, I would very much like to watch a movie with you tonight…alone. It's a date."

A look of relief flashes across his face before turning into his trademark goofy grin.

"Whew, that was a lot harder than I thought it would be. You know you're the first girl I've ever asked out on a date, right? I mean, I once asked Skylar to marry me after she fed me bacon but I don't think that really counts."

I grin teasingly back at him. "Oh, so what you're saying is I'm your second choice?"

He leans toward me. "That depends, do you have bacon?"

A laugh spills out of me and I shove him away.

"I don't know about bacon but if we don't find these missing chickens, eggs will be in short supply!"

We make our way around the perimeter fence without finding any signs of the birds until we walk up to Skylar and Rex who are laying on a blanket together under one of the big trees in one corner of the yard. They look so sweet together and I hate to interrupt them but these missing chickens are driving me crazy so I clear my throat to get their attention.

"Hi, guys. Sorry to interrupt you but we could use your help right now. It seems like we have some missing chickens. You didn't happen to see any wandering around free did you?"

Rex shakes his head but Skylar just looks up at me with a dreamy smile on her face.

"The chickens have flown the coop?" she asks with a laugh.

I can't help it smile back at her. It's really nice to see Skylar happy like this. She deserves it after everything she's been through in her life.

"Yeah, it looks that way," I say. "We've looked everywhere for them and we can't find them."

Rex sits up and looks toward the main building. "Any chance Belle decided that chicken was on the menu tonight? Maybe your missing chickens are in a pot right now!"

I turn and look that way but his words get Skylar's attention causing her dreamy expression to change to one of concern as she pushes herself up into a sitting position too. She shakes her head firmly.

"No, she wouldn't do that. She knows that I'm trying to build up our flock. They have to be around here somewhere."

Marsh shrugs his shoulders. "I don't know, we can't find them anywhere. I checked for any possible hiding places in the cabin and Joslin and I walked the whole perimeter looking for them. Where else could they possibly be?"

Skylar pushes to her feet and reaches down to pull Rex up with her. "We'll go check with Belle to make sure she didn't take them if you guys want to go back to the cabin for another look. Make sure you check the rafters in the roof. You never know, they somehow might have made it up there to perch. How many are missing anyways?"

I blow out a frustrated breath. "Three of the adult hens and three of the baby chicks. I can see maybe the hens making it up to the rafters somehow but there's no way the babies would have. We'll head over there and then meet you guys in the yard once we've checked again and we'll go from there."

We split up, with Marsh and I heading back to the hen cabin for another look but I don't think we're going to find them in the rafters. Even if we do find the hens there, where the heck would the babies have gone?

A quick look inside is all it takes to show me that the hens aren't there so we head over to the main building to see if Skylar's had any better luck. She and Rex come out with the boys hot on their tail. When we meet up, she shakes her head.

"No chickens for supper tonight. Nobody's seen any of them loose so we're going to have to do a better search for them." She purses her lips in an annoyed way and looks around the yard one more time before saying, "We're going to have to walk the perimeter again but this time we'll look for any holes that they might have gone through." She shakes her head. "You watch, it's going to be something stupid like they're under one of the other cabins or something. As much as I enjoy my eggs, chickens can be a royal pain in the butt!" She looks down at Ben and Matty.

"Okay, you two need to be super detectives and help us find our missing birds. I want you to look in every cabin and listen carefully for any squawking or chirping in case they've managed to get underneath one of the cabins. The rest of us will start behind this building and go in separate directions to check for holes in the perimeter fence. We'll all meet back here and hopefully, one of us will find the little buggers!"

Ben and Matty whoop in excitement at the task and take off for the nearest cabin while the rest of us circle around to the back of the atrium building and go our separate ways. Marsh and I go left while Skylar and Rex go right. It doesn't take long for my back to start aching as we walk hunched over along the fence looking for a hole.

After a few minutes of this Marsh asks, "So, what kind of movie do you want to watch tonight? I'm good with watching a chick flick if you want."

I stop for a minute to stretch my back out and spear him with a look. "I'm not really a chick flick kind of girl. I'd rather watch something sci-fi or action if you don't mind."

A grin spreads across his face. "That's awesome! And just so you know, I'm not really a chick flick kind of guy either. I just wanted you to know that I could be okay with one if you wanted."

I laugh at him and ask teasingly, "Marsh, are you trying to tell me that you can be sensitive?"

He looks uncertain for a minute but then nods his head exaggeratingly. "Yep, that's me, Mr. Sensitive. I promise if you ever need a shoulder to cry on, I'm your guy!"

I tap my chin in consideration and then nod. "Well, I guess that's good to know. If I ever feel the need to have a good cry, I'll make sure to find one of your shoulders." I say mockingly.

His cheeks redden in embarrassment causing him to look away before bending over and scanning the base of the fence again. "I just want you to know that, you know, there's more to me than meets the eye. We haven't really had much chance to get to know each other that well so I just..."

When he trails off without finishing the sentence, I reach out and put a hand on his arm. "Relax Marsh, I'm just giving you a hard time. I like you. I mean, I like what I know of you so far."

Now it's my turn to blush in embarrassment so I pick up my pace a little bit until I'm ahead of him and start scanning the fence again. I feel kind of ridiculous. I somehow managed to be a secret agent for seven years and take down an entire bunker full of military soldiers but I'm completely out of my depth when it comes to dealing with the first boy who's ever showed an interest in me. I just hope it gets easier. My only consolation is that he seems just as clueless as me.

By the time we make it all the way around the perimeter fence and meet back up with Skylar and Rex, my back is screaming at me in pain from walking hunched over for so long. None of us have had any luck finding any holes in the fence and the boys are still popping up and down then running from cabin to cabin on their hunt. They're making so much noise that if there are any missing chickens around they'll hopefully scare them out of hiding. Skylar throws up her hands.

"Well, I don't know what else we can do except keep our eyes out for them. They're bound to show up eventually. We'll just have to let everybody else know they're missing and hope someone spots them."

Rex nods his head in agreement. "They're here somewhere. I just hope they didn't get themselves trapped somewhere they can't get out of. It would be a real shame to lose six chickens but I agree, I'm not sure what else we can do except keep an eye out for them."

Skylar looks over at the chicken cabin in annoyance and nods. "Well, looks like our break is over Rex, so I'm going to go over and see if I can figure out which ones are missing. I might have to pull another one of our laying hens so it can brood on a nest. If these idiot chickens are going to kill themselves on a regular basis, then we're going to need lots more baby chicks."

Skylar and Rex head over to the chicken cabin and I turn to go into the building and find Marsh in my way. I give him a brief smile.

"Thanks for your help on the search today. I'll take a look through the movie collection and see what I can come up with for us to watch tonight."

He nods and gives me his goofy grin that doesn't seem so goofy to me anymore. It's kind of charming now.

"Yeah, of course, it was my pleasure. Let me know if there's anything else I can do to help...anytime."

I can't help the silly smile that grows across my face at his adorable awkwardness as I step around him. He's like a cute puppy dog - if puppy dogs had killer cheekbones!

Chapter Fourteen - Skylar

It's late when I finally get the two monkeys settled down for the night. We had spent the evening watching a movie about a board game that transports the player's house into outer space. Every roll of the dice has the players fighting aliens or asteroids and they can't get home until they finish the game. I have to admit, for a kid movie, it was pretty good. The laptops that Joslin had brought with her are lifesavers when it comes to entertainment for the boys. Being able to use the batteries to watch movies instead of running the generator and wasting gas is awesome. I plant a kiss on each of their sleepy foreheads before turning out the light and heading to the door with a soft smile on my face. It was a really nice night sitting with the two little monsters pushed up against me smelling like fresh cut grass and, well, boy. Coming to the camp and building a life here just gets better every day for me after so long living in the bunker.

I leave their door cracked open a few inches in case they need me during the night as I head into my room through the connecting door we built in the wall between the offices. I glance over at my bed for a few seconds before turning away and heading out into the hallway. A glass of milk is on the menu for a bedtime snack. As I walk down the hall, I see Joslin's door is cracked open with the light still on. I can't help myself from glancing through the opening. My steps slow when I see her and Marsh sitting together on the small loveseat we had brought over from the hotel for her room. They're facing each other and talking softly while holding hands. I speed back up again so they don't see me and grin. Looks like I'm not the only one who's happy to be building a life here in the camp.

I go into the kitchen and grab a glass before quickly opening the fridge and pulling out a pitcher of milk and shutting the door just as quickly to keep the cold air in. We only run the generator a few hours a day now to conserve our gas so the appliances have to rely mostly on the solar power we have set up. The kitchen is dimly lit by a few strategically-placed solar lawn lights that we scavenged from the resort grounds. They don't put out a lot of light but there is enough to navigate around the counter and tables in the next room. Every morning we take them back outside and let them charge in the full sun before bringing them back in at nightfall. I head down the hallway back toward my room, this time not pausing at Joslin's door and I'm about to turn in to my doorway when flickering light further down the hallway catches my eye. It looks like someone has a candle lit in the atrium so I head down there to see who is still up.

When I step into the atrium it's much brighter than what a single candle could light up. It's coming from the right side of the room and I stand there confused for a moment trying to figure out what would cause it to be so bright over there. When my brain comes up with the answer the glass of milk drops from my hand and shatters on the concrete floor sending the creamy white liquid and glass shards everywhere. For half a moment I can't get the breath that I need to get out the scream that's building in my chest but then it finally sucks down into my lungs and I let loose as loud as I can.

"FIRE!"

I spin on my heels and run in a sprint back down the hallway screaming "FIRE" at the top of my lungs. I reach out and grab the door frame to my room and use it to propel myself through the opening straight toward the connecting door to the boy's room. I slam it open and it hits the wall behind it with a loud bang causing both boys to shoot up into sitting positions on their beds

"Up, up, up! We need to go outside right now!" When they both immediately throw back the covers and scramble to their feet, I point at generator shed

the floor by their beds. "Shoes! Just slip your feet into them, don't worry about tying them!"

Their faces are filled with fear but they do as I say and I quickly grab them by their hands and lead them out of their room and through mine into the hallway where Marsh and Joslin are standing looking every which way in confusion.

"Joslin! Get the boys out of here. Take them to the playground and keep them there. Marsh, on me! There's a fire outside behind the atrium and we need to grab all the fire extinguishers we pulled from the resort."

Joslin grabs the boy's hands and starts pulling them down the hall toward the exit and I call after her.

"Once you get the boys to the playground, start banging on cabin doors and get everybody else out here to help us!"

She releases Ben's hand for a moment to wave over her head that she heard me so Marsh and I bolt back toward the atrium. We've been using one corner of the big room to stack many of the extra supplies we brought from the bunker as well as all the material and goods we've scavenged from the resort so far. Leaning up against the wall are about ten large red fire extinguishers. It's a roll of the dice whether or not they're going to work after not being serviced for the last seven years, but it's all we have right now so I scoop two up and say a quick prayer that they'll still be useful. With our arms full of the heavy extinguishers, Marsh and I pause and take a good look at the flames that shine through the atrium windows. I swear that they've already doubled in size.

Marsh lets out a harsh curse and I nod my head curtly in agreement before we turn and move as quickly as possible back down the hallway to the exit. We both know that the only thing out there on that side of the building is the storage shed where we've been keeping the generator and most of our extra fuel containers. If we lose all of it, and it looks like that's what's happening, it's going to be a real hit on our options for where we can go in the future.

By the time we stagger under the weight of the extinguishers through the front doors and into the yard, Lance and Ethan are just coming out of their cabin and Joslin's pounding on Rex's door. I drop my two extinguishers on the ground and start waving at Lance and Ethan.

"Over here! The generator shed is on fire!" As soon as I see that they've heard me and they're heading in our direction, I turn and run back into the building to grab two more extinguishers with Marsh hot on my heels. We make two more runs and by the time we get around the atrium and see the fire up close, my arms feel like wet noodles. I'm surprised to see Lance and Ethan just standing between the atrium glass and the shed that's now a blazing inferno. They're not even trying to put out the fire so I drop one of the extinguishers and work frantically at trying to pull the safety wire from the handle of the one that I still have in my arms while screaming at them above the roar of the flames.

"What the frack are you doing? We have to try and put it out!"

Lance turns and looks my way before coming over and pulling the extinguisher from my hands. He has to yell to be heard over the sounds of the fire.

"Skylar! We're not going to be able to put it out. It's being fueled by all that gasoline and even if we had twenty extinguishers, it's too late! We just have to keep an eye on it now and make sure it doesn't spread to any of the other buildings."

I shake my head in denial but the heat that's evaporating the sweat from my face tells me he's right. Without a fire truck or high-pressure water hose, there's no way that blaze is going to be put out. I stand there feeling defeated and watch as our precious supplies burn until an arm reaches around and pulls me back against his chest. Rex uses his other hand to wipe the tears that I didn't even know we're falling from my face. He rests his chin on top of my head and whispers.

"It'll be all right. It's just stuff. All that matters is everyone's safe. The boys are safe and we'll just find a way to carry on."

A soft sob escapes my throat at his words and I let my tense shoulders droop back as I lean against him. He's right, this is a setback but everybody's safe, no one got hurt and that's all that matters. Lance, Ethan, Marsh, Rex and I stand there for a good twenty minutes watching the fire before Belle comes around the corner of the building and interrupts our mourning with a loud gasp.

She drags her eyes from the inferno with a shake of her head and meets mine. "Skylar, I put Ben and Matty back to bed in Rex and Marsh's cabin. They're scared so Joslin and Sasha are staying with them but you two should go talk to them and reassure them that everything's okay."

I nod to her, thankful that she's taken care of the boys and pull away from Rex. I turn to Lance. "Are you okay to watch over this while we go settle the boys down?"

He waves us away. "Yeah, we've got this. There's little wind so I don't expect it to spread much further but we'll keep an eye on it anyways until it dies right down. You guys should try and get some sleep after you talk to the boys. We're going to have to have a long discussion tomorrow about what we're going to do going forward after this."

I close my eyes to try and push back the despair of losing so much gas and then nod at him, Ethan, and Marsh before taking Rex's hand and walking away toward the cabin that the boys are in. When we open the door to the cabin, I've barely taken two steps inside when Benny launches himself at me and begins to sob. Matty's right behind him and crashes into Rex. It takes us over an hour to get them settled down and to convince them that they're safe and that everything will be okay. I pull out every single song I had ever sang to Benny as a baby to get him to finally go to sleep and by the time Rex and I step back out of the cabin my voice is raw and my body vibrates with exhaustion, the adrenaline dumped into my system earlier long gone.

I look over in the direction of the fire but the flames can no longer be seen above the main building. Just a glow is left. I feel like I should go and relieve Lance and the others but I'm just so tired that I find myself sitting down on the steps of the cabin.

Rex lowers himself down beside me and slings an arm around my shoulders and pulls me against him.

"You should go try and get some sleep, Sky. There's nothing you can really do tonight."

I shake my head against him but I know he's right.

"I'm going to stay here and crawl in with Benny. I don't want to be too far away from him right now but I just want to sit here for a minute with you, if that's okay."

He plants a soft kiss on the side of my head and murmurs, "Of course we can."

I turn my eyes away from the glow of the flames and lean back against him so that I can stare up at the stars. Even after a month-and-a-half of seeing them they still give me comfort knowing that the long winter is over and I imagine that my parents are somewhere up there watching over us. I don't know how long we sit there but sometime later as I begin to nod off, Rex pulls me to my feet and takes me back inside and helps me lay down beside Benny without disturbing him. Even though I was almost asleep a few minutes ago on the steps, now that I'm laying in the soft bed with Benny's warm weight against me, I can't sleep. Every time I close my eyes all I see is flames. The idea of all the things that might have happened if I hadn't seen the flicker down the hall or if the fire had spread to the main building keeps me awake. The darkness behind the windows starts to lighten before I finally drift off but it's not a deep sleep. I keep floating in and out until I finally give up when the sun brushes against my face.

I rub at my gritty eyes and take a deep breath causing me to wince at the bitter smell of smoke that coats my skin and clothes. Being careful not to wake up Benny, I slide out of bed. A glance at the other bunks shows me that Matty is sound asleep but Rex is no longer with him so I quietly open the door and leave the cabin.

I stand on the steps and look around the yard in the early morning sunlight. There's wisps of fog or maybe smoke clinging to the ground here and there but the glow from the flames is no longer showing on the other side of the main building. There's just a small trail of smoke floating up into the sky so the fire must be mostly out. I turn away from the sight and step off the stairs and walk over to the hand pump. I need a wake-up jolt of fresh cold water on me before I can even think about facing what needs to be done next. I get the water pumping until it's a steady stream and then just stick my whole head under it. The cold water is exactly what I need to clear the cobwebs from my eyes and mind and remove the ugly smell of smoke from my hair and skin. When my hair is fully saturated I stand up and wring the excess water from it and wipe it from my face. I don't feel like a new girl but I do feel better so I quickly weave the wet strands into a braid and use a strip of fabric from my pocket to tie it off before heading toward the main building.

My steps falter when I see Jackson come around the building from the direction of where the fire was and realize he was the only person I didn't see last night when the flames were roaring. My lips flatten and my eyes turn to slits of anger as I pick up my pace and march toward him. He looks up when I'm just a few paces away from him and his eyes go wide when he sees my expression. My hands reach out and slam into his chest to shove him back.

"Where the Frack were you last night?" I spit at him.

He backpedals a few more feet as he shakes his head quickly. "Skylar, I didn't know. No one woke me up!"

I snarl. "Give me a freaking break! Are you trying to tell me you slept through all the yelling and commotion that happened last night? Or maybe you had a reason to stay away. Got anything you want to confess, Jackson? Maybe a little delayed revenge for what happened with your dad?"

The complete and utter shock on his face dampens my rage slightly but even if he isn't guilty of setting the fire, he is guilty of not being there while the rest of us suffered through witnessing it. Even though Jackson's been apprenticing with Ethan he still hasn't made a huge effort to be a part of our group and it makes him an easy target for my frustration and anger.

He holds up his hands in a stop gesture. "I didn't… Wouldn't…" His face changes from denial to anger and he takes a step toward me. "Frack you, Skylar!"

I clench my fist and get ready to plow it into his face.

Chapter Fifteen - Rex

I step back from the pile of ashes in front of me, wipe my brow and readjust the bandana I have over my nose and mouth. The bitter stench from the remains of the fire causes my eyes to water. Marsh and I have been using rakes to pull the coals into a wider area to try and get them to cool faster. With the gasoline fueling the fire it burned so hot and quickly that there's not much left of the shed and generator except for a few twisted metal parts. I'm just about to start raking again when I hear a yell from out in front of the main building. I turn and see Skylar and Jackson nose to nose and it's clear they're about to come to blows. I toss my rake down and rush toward them. I already have an idea of what this might be about because I had a similar negative thought about Jackson first thing this morning. When I reach them, I stick an arm between the two of them and haul Jackson away from Skylar, putting myself between the two of them. I turn to Skylar and hold up a hand.

"Whoa, whoa! Calm down, Skylar. What's this all about?"

She glares at Jackson over my shoulder while crossing her arms in anger.

"I was just asking Jackson where he was last night. He claims he slept through the whole thing!"

I feel Jackson press up against my back at her sarcastic tone so I turn sideways and use a hand to shove him back with a warning look before turning back to Skylar.

"Sky, I understand why you would think that Jackson might have been involved with the fire because I had the same thought. I went into his cabin this morning to have the same conversation. He was dead asleep with earphones on and had no idea what had happened. He also didn't smell like smoke."

When her face sets into a stubborn scowl I shake my head and say pointedly, "Let it go, Skylar, he didn't have anything to do with it!"

Jackson makes a sound of aggravation causing me to turn back to him. His face has a furious expression on it when he throws his hands up into the air in frustration.

"What the heck is wrong with you guys? I've never done anything to any of you!"

I look at him dispassionately and shrug my shoulders. "You're right, you've never done anything to us but you've also never done anything with us either." At his confused expression, I sigh. "Jackson, trust is earned and not just freely given in this world. You don't spend any time with us. You don't join in our conversations or join us when we play games at night or watch movies together. You've isolated yourself from everyone here except for Ethan. That means we don't know you. If you want us to accept you, then you're going to have to make an effort to be a part of our group more than just working with Ethan in the clinic. If you want us to trust you, then start building some with us."

I turn my back on him and reach out for Skylar's arm to guide her away from him. I understand her reasoning and frustration with him but until he makes more of an effort to have relationships with all of us, he's going to be the odd man out.

It only takes us a few steps before I feel Skylar relax from her angry stance beside me and she sighs deeply.

"I'm sorry, I overreacted."

"Yup, you did," I reply neutrally.

"I totally could have handled that better," she says.

I don't answer other than to make a "mmhmm" noise.

She comes to a stop beside me, forcing me to stop walking too.

"Maybe I should go back and apologize to him?"

I take her arm again to get her moving before replying. "No, you shouldn't. Yes, you overreacted and could have handled it better but it was the same reaction I had when I realized Jackson hadn't been around last night when the fire was going. If he wants to stay here with us, he really needs to start trying to be a part of our group. I'm not talking about just doing the work that we all need to do to keep this place going either. I'm talking about having relationships with us. Having conversations, jokes, fun even. We've all tried to include him at every turn over the last month and none of us except for Ethan has had any success. The bottom line is, we can't trust him if we don't know him and we can't know him if he doesn't let us."

She leans against me so I let go of her arm to put mine around her shoulders.

"Okay, I'll leave it alone for now but I need to apologize to him. It wasn't that long ago that I had my own trust issues and wouldn't integrate into your group." She kicks at a small stone in her path. "This really sucks! Everything was going so well and now we have missing chickens, a destroyed generator, and a huge gas shortage."

I give her shoulders a squeeze in comfort. "Hey, this isn't a game changer for us. It's more like a game tweak instead. We're still living the good life here. We'll just have to change a few things up, that's all."

Just as we reach the doors to the main building, Lance pushes through them. I frown in concern at the pure exhaustion wearing his features down. His eyes are red and swollen from spending the night in the smoke monitoring the fire to make sure it didn't spread to any of the other structures.

"What are you doing up? You need to go get some sleep, man. We got everything under control here. There's nothing left but coals and ash and Marsh is watching over it." I tell him.

He gives me a grim smile. "Yeah, I'll catch a nap in a little while but right now I'd like to get everybody together in the dining room for a meeting. Can you gather everybody up for me and send them in?"

I nod. "Sure, just give me five minutes and I'll get everybody in there."

He gives my shoulder a pat and sends a tired smile Skylar's way before turning around and going back into the building. I've never seen Lance so worn looking before. He's been such a pillar of strength for us for the last seven years that I've never really thought about the toll living in this destroyed world would take on him. I turn and drop a quick kiss on Skylar's forehead and move to go but she stops me.

"Is it just me or is Lance calling a lot of meetings lately?"

I look back at the building with a frown while considering her words and then turn to her.

"Well, they've all been about things we needed to discuss. I think the role of leader is starting to weigh on him a bit. He never seems to stop worrying about the future. Hopefully, things will settle back down again after this and he can relax for a while." I pull away from her. "I'll meet you inside."

"Ok, I'm going to go and check on the boys. They should be waking up any time now and they're going to be looking for us and their breakfast. I'll see you in there." She says and starts walking toward the cabins.

I jog around the corner of the building to find Jackson and Marsh standing a few feet from the burnt-out area leaning on the rakes we had been using to spread the coals.

"Hey guys, Lance has called a meeting in the dining room and he wants us all there." I tilt my head toward the wreckage. "This looks like it's safe now to leave unattended. Let's head in and see what's up."

Marsh pulls the bandana off his face and uses it to wipe some of the soot from his cheeks and forehead before throwing a disgusted look at the pile of ash and cinder.

"Yep, definitely done like a very badly burnt dinner. Just give me a few minutes to soak my head under the pump and I'll be right in."

Jackson doesn't say anything but nods his agreement. I'm sure after the conversation we just had he doesn't have a whole lot to say to me so I just nod back before turning and going to see if Sasha and Belle are up yet. Their cabin is empty so I assume they must already be in either the kitchen or the dining room. Skylar and the two boys meet me halfway across the yard so the four of us head to the dining room together.

Lance and Ethan are sitting at one end of the long table drinking coffee and having a quiet conversation. Joslin's a few feet away from them tapping away at her tablet but she looks up when we come in and gives us a sleepy nod before going back to whatever is on her screen. Skylar waves us into our seats and heads into the kitchen to rustle up some breakfast for the boys. It's quiet in here with just Ben and Matty chatting. Everybody's tired and feeling the effects of the long night with little sleep.

I blink my gritty swollen eyes and wish I had taken the time to stick my own head underneath the hand pump to try and clear away some of the smoke that clings to me while trying to pay attention to whatever the boys are saying. Thankfully, Skylar, Belle, and Sasha come in from the kitchen with large pans of food for breakfast to distract them. I leave the table to go grab a stack of plates and a handful of utensils for everybody and quickly make up a plate for Matty and me while Skylar makes hers and Ben's. I've only taken a few bites when Marsh and Jackson come in and grab their own plates of food. The meal is almost silent with nobody having any conversation including the boys. They've picked up on the tension in the room and keep sending nervous glances our way. I swallow down the bite of biscuit I'm eating and send them both a weary smile of reassurance.

"Everything's okay guys. Everyone's just super tired from being up most of the night. There's nothing for you guys to worry about. We all just need a nap!"

This sends Benny into a fit of giggles causing Skylar to smile my way.

"You guys aren't babies. Only babies nap!" Ben declares.

Marsh leans forward to look down the table at us. "That's not true! I'm a champion napper. I've been known to nap for hours and hours. Just ask my dads!"

The boys erupt in laughter, breaking the tension in the room, as everyone smiles at their reaction and we finish the meal in a better state of mind. As soon as the boys have finished eating, Skylar takes them out of the dining room and gets them set up in their bedroom with a movie on one of the laptops to keep them busy for a little while so we can have our meeting. They're already on edge with the fire last night and everyone's moods this morning so they don't need to be worrying about whatever we talk about at this meeting. Everyone pitches in to do the breakfast dishes and as soon as they're all clean and put away we settle back down at the table.

Lance scrubs at his face before sighing deeply and looking around meeting each one of our gazes.

"I'm not going to lie to you, losing the generator and most of our gas was a real hit to our future plans. The solar panels and windmills will keep the fridge and freezer going but with those as our only power source, we will have to be very conservative with how we use them. What it really affects is our travel plans. We had decided to go scout and scavenge in the city for one, the wood pellets for the stoves we set up and two, for possible relocation options. Right now both the trucks have full tanks of gas in them because we always top them up every time we use them. They also each have one five-gallon can of gas in the back but that's it as far as our fuel goes. That means I don't feel comfortable burning the gas to scope out the city. Getting the wood pellets would have been nice but we can just burn wood instead. It will mean we will all have to step up in that area to make sure we have enough to get us through the winter and we will have to start now to get it done." He pauses to take a drink of his coffee before going on.

"We hadn't made any kind of decision on relocating to the city because we were going to scout it out first so here are our options on that. We can stay here and keep going as we have been. Yes, losing the generator sucks but we went seven years without one and we managed to make it through. The other option is to wait until harvest, then pull everything, get it canned or dried and then loaded up into the trucks and just go for it. We can find a defensible position in one of the buildings in the city and then scope things out on foot. I'm positive there will be a lot of supplies in that city that haven't been touched that would really help us out in the long run. But, we'd be going in blind so we need to take that into consideration."

"As far as staying here, we would only be able to do a few scavenging runs in the area before we would be out of gas and most of this area has been pretty picked over as far as any food goes so there might not even be any point to that. Also, keep in mind if we do stay here and we use up the gas that we have and then something goes really badly wrong, we'd be stuck in place. Other than the resort, there's nothing else out here that we could set up as a defensible shelter. At least in the city, if we were forced to move we'd have more options on where we could go. Even if it was on foot. So there's the pros and cons of both staying and going. I want us all in agreement on what we decide. Let's hear what everybody thinks."

Chapter Sixteen - Joslin

I start running the numbers on my tablet for how much gas we have and how far it will take us while everyone else gives their opinions on whether we should relocate. I listen with one ear to the debate while opening up the folders that I have stored on my tablet with Calgary's data that I had compiled before leaving the bunker. Belle and Sasha are firmly on the stay put side.

"I haven't changed my mind. I just don't think it would be smart to move. We're settled here and comfortable. We put in a lot of work to make this our home. It just doesn't make sense to me to go into the city where we don't know what we can expect or even who we can expect there. We have the wall and the gate here to give us security so we're safe," Belle says.

Lance shakes his head and counters that. "Yes, and again, we have the wall and gate but that doesn't mean we're safe. We don't have enough people to defend this place properly. And yes we did put in a lot of work to make this camp comfortable for us but who knows what winter will bring. We have no idea how long or how harsh it will be. If anything goes wrong here, we would have limited options for finding more supplies or even a new location. The city would give us way more options for both."

Sasha shakes her head violently. "I don't want to leave! I'm tired of everything changing and never knowing what's going to happen next. I want to stay here!"

Lance looks away from her, exasperated with her whining tone. "Rex, Marsh what do you guys think?"

Marsh shrugs. "Honestly, I could go either way. Belle and Sasha are right in that we've put a lot of work into this place and other than the bunker, it's the best setup we've had since this all started. As far as safety goes, we're fairly isolated here so we don't really have to worry about roaming bands of scavengers stumbling on to us. The wall and gate do give us a level of protection but you're right, Dad, when you say that we don't have enough people to defend this place if we were hit by a group of people. We have very few options for what we can scavenge around here especially now that we have limited gas so I'm fine if we stay but I'm also open to relocating to the city where we have more opportunities. The bottom line is, we can go around and around on this issue but it's pretty equal either way so we just need to make a decision and do it."

Lance nods and looks to Rex for his opinion. Rex mimics Marsh's shrug.

"I'm with Marsh. I'm good to stay but I'm also good to go." He turns to Skylar. "What do you think, Sky? What do you want to do?"

When Skylar doesn't answer right away I look up from my tablet and find her staring at me so I raise my eyebrows in a "what?" expression. She frowns at me and turns to Lance.

"I like the idea of staying here after all the work we put into the place but I don't like not having more options due to the gas issue so can't we try and find more gas?"

I answer her question before Lance has a chance to. "No, that's not possible anymore. I mean, there's gas out there that we could find but it would be too degraded to be useful at this point. Like I said at the last meeting, we could add a ton of stabilizers and additives to it so that it might work for a while but in the end, it would destroy any engines we use it in and that's not a chance I think we want to take with most vehicles out of commission now."

She stares hard at me with a frown on her face that confuses me. It's almost like she expects something else from me and I don't understand what so I just shake my head at her and turn back to Lance.

"By my calculations, we have enough gas to drive to the city and scout out the westernmost edge of it, drive back here load everything up and then go back to our chosen location. That will take all of the fuel in our tanks - leaving us with the five-gallon spare cans as our only remaining supply. As far as scouting the city on foot, that is not an option or at least not much of an option. The city of Calgary encompasses over three hundred square miles and at the time of the bombing the population was one point three million. It had quite a sprawl so trying to cover that much ground on foot would just not be possible. I do have some overview photos that I downloaded from the satellites as well as some maps of the city that we could go over to give us an idea of what's where so that we wouldn't have to waste time or fuel driving around."

Lance nods his head in thoughtful consideration before asking, "So you think we should go then?"

I shake my head. "I didn't say that. I'm just giving you the data so that we can all make an informed decision. Something else to consider, if we decide to stay here, I would suggest we make the short run to the closest ski hill and look for chains for our tires. I do know that there can be a large amount of snowfall traditionally in this area so driving on the roads will become almost impossible once full winter hits. If we can get chains for the tires and even possibly a plow attachment for the cargo truck, we would have more options should something occur during the height of winter that forces us to leave."

I set my tablet down on the table in front of me and look around at everyone at the table before continuing. "I've always been open to finding a different location for our permanent home. The only reason I picked this camp in the first place was because of its proximity to the bunker and the ease of transferring supplies without anyone realizing what we were doing. I think relocating to the city has a lot of potential for us but whatever we find there will need a considerable amount of work to set up so that we have the ability to grow crops over the winter as well as for defense. Because of the lack of fuel, we will only have one shot at finding the right location for us and then we will have a lot of work ahead of us. I'm expecting winter to come early so that means we have at best one month to accomplish everything we need to before the cold weather sets in. I would recommend that we save the fuel for now and in the spring once the snow melts make the move."

Lance looks around at everyone sitting at the table and receives nods of agreement. "All right then, it's settled. We'll stay here for the winter and then come spring, we look to relocate to the city. That's some good advice, Joslin, about the tire chains and plow attachment. We shouldn't have any problem finding those things at the ski hill down the road. You said there was no one occupying it when you sent the drone overhead, right?"

When I shake my head, he goes on. "So, the two most important things we will have to achieve between now and the beginning of winter is to make a run to the ski hill and start chopping more wood. Now that we're not going in to get pellets for the stoves we brought back and installed, we're going to have to step up our wood chopping considerably to get us through the winter without freezing to death. We will have to move everyone into this building as well as the animals. There's just no way we'll be able to cut enough wood to heat multiple structures. It's going to be crowded and by the end of winter it's going to be smelly, but we'll survive," he says with a smile.

Rex pushes back from the table, gets to his feet and points at Lance. "There, it's settled, now you need to go grab a shower and catch some shut-eye. You look exhausted. Take a break, Lance. Marsh and I will head out and start downing some trees this afternoon. We can work on sectioning them tomorrow."

I'm slightly surprised when Jackson pushes to his feet as well. "I'll join you guys."

I see the subtle signs of surprise on both Marsh and Rex's faces and feel relief that Jackson is finally starting to try and include himself in more activities with the others. Hopefully he will put even more effort into it. Otherwise, it's going to be a long and tense winter with us all stuck in this building.

Lance laughs but it's clear just how tired he is when he nods in agreement, gets up and slowly leaves the room without giving his usual list of cautions to the boys, even though they're going to be leaving the fenced area. I look to Ethan in concern but when he meets my gaze he just nods reassuringly.

"He's okay. He's just tired. Things have been going so well here and he started to let his guard down a little bit so the fire put him in a bad frame of mind. He just needs to get some sleep. He'll be back to himself soon enough." He pushes away from the table and stands. "I think I'll go take another look at the herbal remedies you downloaded for me. With all of us in this building with the animals this winter I want to make sure we have a good supply for any coughs and colds that might pop up." He turns to the boys. "You all make sure to stay safe out there!"

Belle and Sasha leave the table and head back into the kitchen and it's easy to tell that they're both relieved that we won't be leaving here anytime soon. Rex, Marsh and Jackson head out leaving just me and Skylar at the table. I pin her with a look.

"Is there something you want to say to me? You've been giving me weird looks for the past little while and I have no idea what it's about."

She doesn't answer me right away. Instead, she looks down at the table and runs her thumbnail along a groove made by some long-ago summer camper. When she finally looks up at me her face is filled with indecision.

"Look, I didn't want to say anything in front of the others because I don't really know what your game plan is here but why can't we just go back to the bunker to get more gas? I'm sure there's no one left up there by now so we could just go and get what we need and come back."

I shake my head in confusion. "What are you talking about? The bunker is shut down. There's no way for us to get in there and get to any of the supplies."

She cocks her head to the side and gives me a look of annoyance. "We both know that's not true. You made the soldiers and everyone else think that she was self-destructing but AIRIA is up and running just fine. Don't misunderstand me, I like living out here under the sun and I don't want to go back to living inside that mountain but there's no reason why we can't go and get the things we need from there and bring them back."

I just stare at her in surprise. I don't know if she's deluding herself because she can't accept AIRIA's demise or if she really thinks that I was bluffing, but this isn't healthy. She has to accept that AIRIA is gone.

I put as much compassion into my tone as I can when I say, "Listen, Skylar. I know AIRIA was like a parent to you, a lifeline even, but this is unhealthy. You need to let her go. She's not coming back. She can't help us anymore."

Her expression shifts to surprised amusement. "You think I'm delusional? Really? You really think that I just can't accept that she self-destructed?"

At my slow nod, Skylar burst out laughing. I just sit and wait for her to come to her senses and when she does she shocks the heck out of me at what she says next.

"AIRIA is up and running...period. A month and a half ago I had a little mini funeral for her where I buried my communicator to say goodbye. Imagine my surprise when the fracking thing starts talking to me and asking if I was in distress! I don't know what you did to make it look like you shut her down but it didn't work!"

My mouth is hanging open in shock at this and my mind is going a million miles a minute to try and figure out how that could be possible. If what Skylar is saying is true, that means AIRIA found a way around my virus and did a reset somehow back to before we took Skylar's clearance away from her. When I uploaded the virus, AIRIA wouldn't even communicate with Skylar because of her red clearance level so if her communicator was working and AIRIA was addressing her that means she's somehow reset herself to before the General took control of her systems.

I finally refocus on Skylar and shake my head slowly in awe. "Do you know what this means? This is a game-changer for us. With access to everything in that bunker and AIRIA herself, we could go back and implement the plans that you and the others had come up with before the General showed up. We could get more people and really start to rebuild this time without that lunatic threatening us. Oh, my God, this is amazing!"

Skylar throws her hands up in the air. "Whoa, whoa, who said anything about getting more people? I'm just talking about going and getting some supplies, some more gas. I did that whole 'taking in the refugees' thing and it didn't turn out that great for us. I like it here and I like the dynamic between, well, most of us. Scaling up the rebuilding effort like you're talking about, that's something I'd really have to think about."

I nod my head in understanding but I'm distracted by all the plans and options we could have now. "Sure, sure, we could talk about it, think about it. But seriously Skylar, think about everything we could do with AIRIA and the bunker under our control again. We need to tell the others."

She shakes her head quickly. "I don't know. I can already see how that'll go. Half of them are going to want to go straight back to that place and give up this camp. It was my home for seven years and it protected me and Benny but now that I've been out here for a couple of months, I can see how living in the bunker was just existing. Living out here in the world, building something, growing things under the sun and sky, this… this is really living. I don't know if I want to give that up."

I feel the smile growing across my face. "That's just it, Skylar, you don't have to give it up. It wouldn't be like before when you were trapped inside and you couldn't go outside because of the radiation. We'd be able to come and go as we please. We should just go back for the winter and then in the spring we could move outside again. Think about it, we would have access to all the bunker supplies and protection but also be able to be outside whenever we wanted. It would be the same thing as staying here this winter, just a heck of a lot more comfortable. We're going to be trapped in this building for a good portion of the winter and yes we'll be able to go outside now and again when the weather isn't too bad but while we're stuck inside this building it's going to be uncomfortable no matter how much wood we chop. There's two very, very important things in the bunker that should make this decision easy for you."

Skylar arches an eyebrow. "Really? And what is that?"

My smile gets even bigger when I say, "Central heating and hot water on demand!"

She laughs while shaking her head. "Okay, I'll admit that that's a pretty convincing argument you have there but I'd like to just think about it for a while before telling the others. Can you give me that?"

I nod my head eagerly. "Of course! Take your time and really think it over but I know you're going to come to the same conclusion as me. Going back is the best option for us. We will be able to do so much more than we can now with what we have and where we're at."

I push my chair away from the table and stand. "I think I'll join Belle and Sasha in the kitchen for a while." She arches her brows at me in amusement. "Don't laugh, they've been giving me cooking lessons. I hope one day I'll be able to master not burning water!"

Skylar grins even wider. "Yeah, you keep working on that. I got to go get the boys on some school work before they become screen zombies."

I watch her as she walks across the room and out the door, marveling at the fact that she sat on the secret of AIRIA being functional for well over a month. I look around the dining room where we've eaten our meals for the past couple of months and smile. I'm actually kind of glad she never told me before this because I might have tried to convince them all to go back sooner and then I would have missed out on what it was like to live here with my family, in our home.

Chapter Seventeen - Rex

Before heading to the gate that Ethan is holding open for us Marsh, Jackson and I grab a few axes and saws to pile into a landscaping cart that we had brought over from the resort. We head left and follow the wide path into the forest toward the cleared area where we've been taking our wood from. Lance has been taking Marsh and me on wood chopping expeditions for years so we give Jackson a rundown on safety as we walk.

"You always want to make sure you know where the tree you're working on is going to fall and make sure you're on the right side of it. We've been working in this area since we got here so there's space to drop them safely without them getting hung up. We'll bring down five or six today and trim off all the branches for now. Tomorrow, everyone will come out and we will section them off to bring them back into the camp with the ATV so we can split and stack them. We're going to have to do this over and over again for the next few weeks to make sure we have enough split wood stored to get us through the majority of winter so I hope you're good with sore shoulders and blistered hands." I tell him with a smile.

Marsh groans. "Oh man, remember the first time we did this back after the bombs dropped? I thought my arms were going to fall off after the first day he had us chopping." He laughs. "My palms were shredded from the ax handle and I thought Ethan was going to blow his top at dad."

I laugh along with him and turn back to Jackson. "Well at least you're not a scrawny eleven-year-old with next to no muscle so maybe it won't be so hard on you." When he just nods tentatively I try and keep the conversation going. "Thanks for coming out here with us. It'll be nice having another set of arms around to make the work go faster." When he just nods again without speaking I bite back a sign of frustration that wants to come out and try a different approach to get him to open up. "So you never really gave your opinion on relocating at the meeting. How do you feel about the subject?"

He shoots a quick glance Marsh's way and meets my eyes briefly before focusing ahead again. "I don't really care, honestly. I mean, it would be pretty interesting to see what's happening in the city and as far as supplies go, I'm sure we'd be able to find more there than out here. Other than that, it just doesn't really matter to me either way."

I glance over at Marsh who just shrugs his shoulders and rolls his eyes. Trying to get Jackson to have any type of conversation with us is like pulling teeth so I throw up a hand to get them to stop. After what happened this morning with Skylar and him and the things I said, I need to nip this in the bud right away. The guy's had long enough to figure out his place in the group and whether or not he wants to be a part of it.

"Jackson, I'm trying to make an effort here but it's not going to work unless you give a little bit back. It was a good first step you volunteering to come with us but you've got to communicate with us, buddy. The only way we're all going to get to know each other better and start forging the bonds of trust is if we talk to each other," I say to him in the most compassionate tone I can rustle up.

He turns to me with a scowl on his face. "What do you want from me? I told you I don't care if we stay or go. What else do you want me to say?" He throws his head back to stare up at the sky for a minute before the tension in his body flows away and he drops his head. His tone of voice borders on weary. "I don't know how to do this, okay. I was surrounded by soldiers who didn't want to hear my voice or my opinions for years. Every time I'd offered an opinion or try to have a conversation, I was shot down or looked down on because I was a kid. The only person I've been able to have real conversations with since I was eleven years old is Joslin. So I'm sorry if I'm having a hard time getting into your buddy banter but it's honestly because I don't know how. If that doesn't fit into your perfect group dynamic then maybe I should just leave."

His words make me see him in a different light that I hadn't even thought to consider, making me fumble my response.

"That's...I...crap! Listen, man, I'm sorry. I had no idea you were so isolated from your father and his men. But that right there is just the kind of thing you need to share with us so that we can start to get to know you."

Marsh starts walking backward down the trail away from us with a goofy grin on his face.

"Yeah man, see, now we know you need to learn good-natured buddy smack talk. I'm totally open to giving you lessons! Let's start right now. If you two Shirleys are done talking about your feelings, there's some timbering to..."

His sentence ends in a scream of agony and he drops to the forest floor. I've never heard anything like the sounds of agony that are coming from my best friend and I'm standing frozen in complete shock trying to figure out what the heck is going on. The sight of Jackson, rushing toward Marsh, who's rolling around on the ground screaming - knocks me out of my confusion and I lunge toward him as well.

When I see what's causing him so much pain I almost have to turn and puke right there.

There's a huge metal animal trap embedded in his lower leg. The teeth on the trap have to be at least two inches long and knowing that multiple teeth are embedded in my friend's leg is sickening. Jackson grabs and lifts Marsh's leg causing him to scream again even louder. He tries to pry the trap open to release Marsh's leg but he can't get it. I'm kneeling beside him with my hand hovering over his leg trying to figure out where to grab or pull when I finally find my voice and yell.

"Leave it! We need to get him inside to Ethan. We have no way of knowing what that trap has punctured inside his leg. If we pull it open he could bleed out if it hit a main artery or vein. We need to get him up and into the cart so we can get him back to the camp."

Marsh's screams have tapered off into agonizing grunts of pain as I run my hands over the trap looking to see if it's connected to a chain. I find the links and give a tug on them and breathe out a sigh of relief that the end of the chain isn't connected to anything like a stake driven into the ground or a nearby tree. I take the chain and wrap it around Marsh's leg so it won't drag and cause even more tension on his wounds.

Jackson rushes to the cart we had been pushing and turns it to point back toward the camp before backing it up next to Marsh. He throws the saws and axes that were in the cart out onto the forest floor before coming to stand on the other side of Marsh. He looks at me and swallows with a gulp.

"Are you ready to do this?" I can see the fear and concern in his eyes when he looks down at Marsh and then back up to me.

I nod slowly and then focus down at my friend. "Marsh, Marsh look at me!"

There's so much pain in his eyes when he finally turns his head my way that I feel tears welling up into my own in sympathy. I shove them back and try and keep my voice steady.

"Okay, you're going to be fine. We're going to take you back to the camp so Ethan can fix you right up and get that thing off your leg. But first, we need to get you into the cart. Buddy, I'm not going to lie to you, this is going to hurt a lot."

Marsh clenches his teeth until his expression looks like an animal snarling and grits out, "Do it! Just do it!"

Jackson kneels down on the other side of him and we both get a tight grip under Marsh's arms before heaving him up to his feet. I have to force myself to ignore his cries of agony because I know the longer this takes the more pain he's going to experience. We both get a hand underneath his thighs to lift him over and into the bed of the cart being careful not to jam his leg up against the side of it. By the time we've got him settled in, he's delirious and incoherent from the pain the movement caused him.

"All right. Jackson, you guide the front and I'll push from behind. We'll go as fast as we can but we don't want to tip the cart."

He gives me a scared nod and then focuses on keeping the front end of the cart straight as I push. I'm so thankful that we hadn't made it very far down the path into the forest when this happened so we don't have as far to go to get back to the gate. As soon as we leave the trees I send Jackson ahead to start yelling for someone to open the gate for us because the path the rest of the way is fairly level and I don't have to worry as much about the cart tipping. I can't stop myself from glancing down at Marsh's face every few seconds. I think he's fallen unconscious because he's not making those horrible painful noises anymore and I think that's a good thing. If he's unconscious, he won't be feeling the pain from every bump and jolt the cart makes.

I catch up to Jackson fairly quickly and stand at the closed gate while he pounds on it and screams at the top of his lungs for someone to come and open it up for what feels like an eternity. I lean over Marsh while we wait and check his pulse and then the wound itself which has a pool of blood collecting under it in the bottom of the cart. Cursing myself for being a panicked idiot, I do what I should have done right from the start and whip off my shirt and use it to wrap around the wound to try and contain the bleeding. It only takes seconds for the fabric to become saturated with Marsh's blood so I undo my belt and pull it free from its loops and use it to create a tourniquet just above where the trap is embedded in his leg. That's the extent of my first aid knowledge so all I can do now is hope that somebody opens the damn gate soon so we can get him to Ethan.

I'm about to start screaming alongside Jackson when I hear the thick board we used to secure the gate scrape against the wood so instead, I race back behind the cart and get ready to push it through as fast as I can. When the gate finally swings open, it's Lance standing there with a confused sleepy expression on his face that quickly morphs into horror when he sees his son in the cart. When he just stands there in the way I start to yell.

"Lance, get out of the way! We need to get him to the clinic right away. We need to get him to Ethan!"

He flinches and backs up a few steps, which is all the room I need to push the cart through the gateway and past him toward the main building. Jackson sprints past me to get the door open and yell down the hallway for help while I can hear Lance's pounding footsteps following behind us. We've barely made it into the hallway when everyone converges on us. Skylar comes flying down the hallway with Ben and Matty on her heels from the direction of their rooms. Belle and Sasha rush out of the dining room but are quickly pushed aside by Ethan who takes one look at his son in the cart and starts barking orders.

"Everybody get out of the way! Rex, straight into the clinic, no stopping. Jackson, I'm going to need you with me to assist. Move! Move! Move!"

Everyone either scatters back into rooms off of the hallway or flattens themselves against the walls so that I can get the cart past them and into the clinic that Ethan has set up in one of the offices. As soon as the cart comes to a stop beside the table he has set up for treatment, he shoves me out of the way so that he can get Marsh's vitals. Once he has what he needs, he stands back up, brushes a loving hand over Marsh's hair, swallows hard and then looks from Jackson to me.

"Okay, we need to get him out of this cart and onto the table. I'd like you two to do the heavy lifting while I keep his leg stabilized."

As soon as we're both in place he counts us down. "All right, on three. One, two, three."

I hadn't even realized Lance had followed us into the room until he pulls the cart out of the way once Jackson and I have taken Marsh's weight off of it. As soon as we lay Marsh gently onto the table, Jackson and I back out of the way so Ethan can go to work. We stand there quietly as he uses sharp scissors to cut the pant leg off of Marsh's wounded leg, waiting for any instructions he might give us to help. He studies the wound closely and then starts running his hands over and around the trap before turning to face us.

His glance meets Lance and holds there for a few seconds. I can see them communicate silently, as only a long-married couple can, before he looks our way and speaks.

"I can't see a lever mechanism to release the tension and spring the trap back open so we're going to have to pry it apart. Ideally, we will pull it apart in one smooth motion and then get it off his leg. I don't want the metal teeth inside his leg sawing back and forth as we try and remove it. That will just cause even more damage. This is how I want to do it. Rex I want you at the end of the table. We're going to lift Marsh's leg about a foot off the table and I want you to brace his foot flat against your stomach and keep it immobilized. Lance and Jackson, I want you two to pry apart the trap and then you'll have to hold it open. I'm going to support Marsh's leg with a hand underneath his calf. Once the trap is open, I will give the word and Rex, you will push the leg toward me carefully so his knee will bend - moving it out of the trap. Lance, Jackson, be very careful you don't let the trap closed again before the leg is out of the way and watch Rex's hand as well. Also, make sure you don't get your own hands snagged in it. I can only work on one patient at a time!" He tries a half-hearted joke.

When no one even cracks a smile he focuses back on his son and counts us down again. Thankfully, it goes smoothly. We get the evil piece of metal off of Marsh's leg without doing any more damage to it or us. As soon as everything is clear, they allow it to slowly close again. Lance throws it down on the floor in disgust.

A breath of relief whooshes out of Ethan. "All right, good work guys. Now I need you to back out of the way so Jackson and I can get to work on him. Jackson, get some gloves on and grab all the sterile solution we made. We're going to need to clean out each one of these wounds to make sure there's no dirt or pieces of fabric lodged in them before we can start stitching them up." He leans over the leg and mumbles under his breath as he works, "What I wouldn't give for a proper operating area not to mention an x-ray machine to check and see if his bone was fractured."

I lean against the wall and look away from what they're doing to meet Lance's exhausted, worried eyes. I can tell he wants to ask what happened so I just launch right into it.

"We've walked that path at least twenty times or more since we settled here. Any of us could have sprung it at any time." I rub my face in frustration before dropping my hands to my sides and shaking my head. "I can't believe this! It's like we're cursed all of the sudden. First, we lose some chickens, then the generator and gas go, and now this!"

A harsh gasp from the doorway has both Lance and me looking that way to find Joslin standing there. I know her and Marsh have been feeling each other out in a relationship so this is going to be hard on her. The weird thing is, she's not looking at Marsh in horror but at the trap on the floor. When she lifts her eyes away from it and meets mine, I see pure panic in them.

"No, not cursed. Sabotage! This isn't bad luck at all. I've… We've seen this before. This trap, this trap came from the back of one of the military trucks we left back at the bunker. Someone's found us and they're toying with us!"

Chapter Eighteen - Joslin

L ance is across the room in a split second to grab my arm and give it a shake.

"What are you talking about? That trap could have been left in place from before the bombs dropped!"

I shake my head in denial. "No, I'm telling you, someone's found us! Think about it, they came over the wall to scout us out and couldn't resist taking some of the chickens. Then they start the fire that takes out our main power source and fuel. Now this! It makes perfect sense. I know it's true! For the past few days I've felt edgy and tense. I think it's because they've been watching us and I felt it."

Everyone is looking at me with doubt, so I continue, almost choking with the urgency I feel. "Listen to me! On our way here from the East, the General stopped at every sign of survivors. We were going through northern Ontario when we saw signs of cook fires in the distance. He sent a team of scouts to check it out and only three of them came back. Two of them came back carrying the third who had that exact trap on his leg! Our doctor had to amputate the injured soldier's leg when infection set in, but it didn't matter in the long run, he died. The General kept the trap because he said it might be useful in the future."

Lance stares hard at me for a few seconds before turning his head to look at Marsh on the table and then whips it back toward Rex.

"Gather the others and let them know what might be happening. Bring the two little ones back here. Then, weapons! Everyone needs to load up on weapons and ammo. If what she says is true, then now is the perfect time for them to hit us while we're distracted with Marsh's injury. You, me and Skylar need to get out to the fence. Two up in the lookout towers, one walking patrol of our perimeter." He turns and speaks to Ethan's back. "As soon as you can free up Jackson, I'm going to need him out there as well."

When Ethan just waves a hand without turning around, Lance turns toward the door with a grim expression. I step forward into his path.

"What about me? I have training. I could help out there!"

He shakes his head. "No, I want you to arm yourself and stay here to protect this room and the boys. Who knows if they've breached us already. If they're coming after us they could already be inside the fence hiding in any of the cabins or even hiding in this building waiting to strike!"

He's about to step past me when there's a huge crash and the building shakes around us and dust rains down from the ceiling. Lance, Rex and I all immediately crouch down and when I look toward Marsh I see both Ethan and Jackson leaning over him to protect him from any falling debris that might come. I turn back toward the doorway ready to launch myself out of it to go check on the others when a second huge crash hits us causing me to drop to the floor.

Lance and Rex both clamp an arm on either side of me and pull me back up to my feet. After another quick look toward Marsh to make sure he's okay, Lance coughs away the dust in his throat.

"This is it! Whatever those two crashes were they came from the atrium. We need to get to the others and start forming up a defense before they walk in here and take us all out!" He yells, before flying out the door.

Rex and I are hot on his heels out of the room but instead of following Lance toward the front of the building, Rex turns to the right and takes two steps before coming to a quick stop. I look in that direction and find my mouth dropping open at what I see. The end of the hallway is completely blocked with tree branches and debris. Quickly, I come to the conclusion that whoever is attacking us somehow managed to cut down at least two of the huge trees just outside the fence and direct their descent onto our building. The atrium must be completely destroyed but what concerns both Rex and me is that the damage debris and tree branches extend into the hallway and through the rooms that Skylar and the boys have been using as their own.

I get moving faster than Rex and I give him a small shove to get him moving until we're both racing toward what's left of the offices to check to see if anyone is in there. The door to Skylar's room is completely impassable with debris and branches so Rex spins on his heel and pushes his way past me to the door leading into the boy's room that we've kept locked. He's about to lift his leg to kick it in when his name is yelled from down the hallway.

We both turn to see Skylar racing toward us hauling both the boys by their arms. She looks past us at the damaged hallway and her face goes white in shock. When she reaches us, Matty throws himself sobbing against Rex. Rex uses one hand to grip him around the shoulders and another to reach out and pull Skylar and Ben against him briefly.

I'm relieved to see that they're all okay but we need to move so I interrupt them. "Guys! Come on we have to go! We're being attacked, Skylar. The boys need to go into the clinic with Ethan and Jackson and you two need to get outside to back up Lance!"

Rex lets go of Skylar with a nod of agreement. "Yes, you're right. Come on boys, I need you to stay in the clinic with Ethan and don't leave no matter what happens or what you hear unless he tells you otherwise. Bad guys are attacking us so it's important you do as he says." When their little faces fill with terror, he tries to assure them. "Don't worry, we're going to stop them!"

I rush past the clinic's open door as Rex and Skylar go inside with the boys. I don't even let myself look to see how Marsh is doing as I race down to the storage closet we've been using for an armory. The door is standing wide open telling me that Lance has already been and gone as I run in and start grabbing as many rifles as I can. We're all carrying handguns and holsters but this battle is going to need more than that if we have any hope of winning. I stuff my pockets with extra pre-loaded magazines and once I'm out of space in my pockets I run back out and down the hall toward the clinic. Skylar and Rex run out and meet me partway there and quickly relieve me of half my load. Rex pushes past me and dashes toward the front door but Skylar stops and puts a hand on my shoulder and squeezes hard.

"Nobody gets past you! Joslin, I'm trusting you to protect him with your life."

I don't have time to answer her because just then the first gunshots ring out from the front of the building and she shoves past me and runs toward them. She yells at Rex who's standing beside the glass front door trying to peek around the frame.

"Go out low and don't stop moving until you find shelter!"

He glances back and nods once before crouching, shoving the door open and disappearing from my view.

This is moving so fast and I can feel my hands shaking. It's one thing to train with other soldiers at the firing range but a completely different thing to actually be in a real-life gun battle. I watch Skylar slip through the front door and out of sight and stare at the closed door for a minute before turning away and moving into the clinic's entrance where I plant my feet half in, half out. This is my post. I won't leave here until this is over. My head feels like it's on a swivel as I track from the front door at the end of the hallway to back into the room where Ethan and Jackson's hands are moving so quick over Marsh's leg that they almost seem to be blurred. My head swings back to the front door when the gunfire intensifies out there. I keep my eyes on the door, expecting any moment for some stranger to burst through and open fire as Ethan gives Jackson instructions inside the room.

"Okay, that'll have to do for now. I've stitched all the main bleeders but we're not going to have time right now to stitch up all these wounds. Hand me the glue, I'll just close them temporarily and bandage his leg up until this is over. You need to get out there and back up everyone else. I can do the rest myself. And Jackson…be careful out there!"

I glance into the room and see Jackson removing the sterile gloves he was wearing and tossing them into a trash can before grabbing one of the rifles I had left in the room for him. He meets my gaze and I have to take a step back from the pure fury I see in his eyes.

"Why can't he just leave me alone?" he asks me through gritted teeth.

I shake my head in confusion. "What are you talking about? Who?"

"My father! You know it's him. Somehow he survived and now he's come after me."

"No, no Jackson! This might be some of his soldiers but it's not him. He's dead! They killed him in that bunker when they found out what he did to their families."

He shakes his head as the fury leaves his eyes, replaced with an expression of resignation on his face and then pushes past me into the hallway. "You're wrong. He'll never let me go until I kill him myself."

As I watch him head toward the front door I feel my heart break for my best friend. He's so tortured by what his father was and did that I don't know if he'll ever be able to come back from it.

These thoughts flee my mind when the gunfire intensifies outside to epic proportions and the hallway fills with sunlight as the front door ahead of Jackson swings open. I can't see past him to see who has come in but Jackson's one-word shout full of rage tells me it's not one of the good guys.

"Matthias!"

I feel my blood go cold when I recognize the name as one of the General's worst soldiers. I can't see past Jackson to take a shot at the guy but I have no problem hearing his taunting words to Jackson.

"Ha! It's the prodigal son! I told you I'd find you one day without the protection of your daddy. Today's the day!"

I can see the rigid tension in Jackson's shoulders and back at Matthias's threatening words but his tone is completely calm.

"My father is not with you?"

Matthias laughs bitterly. "What, you didn't know? Your old man bought it back at the bunker when your little sidekick sold him out with that video she put up. Oh yeah, they tore him apart like a pack of hyenas! Thankfully, we still had a strong leader to fill the void he left. What? Don't look so surprised. We would have tracked you down eventually, you just made it faster by driving right past where we were set up at the growing fields. It wasn't too hard to track you back to this place after that. We've been staying next door at the resort for the last few days watching you all playing your pathetic game of house. Sorry to tell you, but game over!"

He's barely spoken the last word before they unleash on each other and bullets start flying through the hallway. I don't have any choice but to throw myself into the clinic to avoid being shot by a random bullet that Matthias is firing at Jackson. By the time I've picked myself up off the ground, silence has descended once again except for the sounds of Ben and Matty crying. I send a quick worried glance Ethan's way before edging up to the door and peeking around it to see what's happening. A choked sob escapes my throat when I see both Jackson and Matthias down at the end of the hallway on the floor covered in blood.

I ease out the door and cautiously make my way toward them, keeping my rifle trained on Matthias's unmoving body. When I reach Jackson, I kneel beside him while keeping my eyes on Matthias as I reach down to place two fingers on Jackson's neck to search for a pulse. When I can't find one, I force myself to stand up again and unload four shots into Matthias's body to make sure he's dead too.

I back slowly away from the bodies with my rifle pointed firmly at the front door of the building. I can feel the sobs building in my chest but I have to clamp down hard on them because this isn't over yet. There's no more gunfire coming from outside but I know in my gut more is coming and I can't afford to mourn Jackson yet.

I'm halfway back toward the clinic door when the word "YOU!" is barked harshly behind my back. I freeze in place for a split second and then slowly turn around to face The General's second-in-command, Donnelly.

His face is an ugly mask of hate and there's a scar that runs from the corner of his eye to his mouth, dragging one side of his features down. I'm guessing he got that souvenir back in the bunker before he managed to somehow get away. If his eyes alone could set something on fire then I would be burning to ash right now there's so much fury in them.

"You! You did this! He trusted you and you betrayed him and all of us and then ran away like a coward! I'm going to…"

His head rocks back as a hole appears in his forehead before his body topples to the floor. I turn slowly around and see Skylar standing there with her gun still pointed past me. She meets my eyes and drops her arms to her sides with a shake of her head.

"This isn't the movies, Joslin. Bad guys don't get monologues. They just get dead!"

Chapter Nineteen - Skylar

Ethan sticks his head out of the clinic doorway and glances at the dead body almost at his feet before turning and looking in the other direction but Joslin and I are in his way and he doesn't see that Jackson is down there on the floor. I don't tell him because there's nothing he can do for him now. When I went past Jackson, his sightless eyes were fixed on the ceiling so I know he didn't make it. I had to push the guilt of it down deep to stay focused on the threats still ahead of us and I need Ethan to do the same. He turns his gaze to me.

"What's happening out there?" he asks, with an edge of panic in his voice.

"Don't worry, Lance and Rex are fine. We only saw or engaged three guys out in the yard and we took out two of them. I saw the third soldier come in here but it looks like Jackson took care of him. Lance and Rex are doing a search inside the fence and through all the cabins to make sure there isn't anybody else lurking around waiting to take a shot at us." I point at the body on the floor in front of us. "Where did this guy come from?"

Joslin looks down at the dead guy and then further down the hallway toward where the atrium was. "He must have somehow found a way through from there. He didn't come in the front door so he must have climbed in through the broken windows and then found a path between the branches. There could be more in there!"

I give a sharp nod. "Okay, back into the clinic Ethan. Joslin, stay here on guard just in case there's more of them and they make it past me. I'm going to go see if I can get in there and check it out."

When I step toward the atrium it opens Ethan's view to further down the hallway where Jackson lays and he makes a grunt of shocked pain.

Joslin moves into his way blocking him from rushing down the hallway and holds up a hand. A quick glance shows me her eyes are full of tears but she's holding them at bay for now.

"He's gone, Ethan. I already checked him. I couldn't find a pulse." When he just shakes his head and makes a move to go around her, she blocks him again. "You need to go back into the clinic and watch over the boys and Marsh. There's nothing you can do for him now. You have to wait until we've secured the area before you go to him."

He opens his mouth like he's going to dispute that but then snaps it shut, turns and goes back inside the clinic without a word. I reach over and give her arm a squeeze in sympathy for her loss but she just nods her head brusquely and resumes her post in the doorway of the clinic. I head down the hallway toward the atrium and I can see right away how the dead guy managed to slide through the branches. I sling my rifle over my back and pull my handgun from its holster instead. I don't know if there's anyone else waiting for me in that disaster area but the last thing I need while picking my way through it is to get my rifle tangled in these branches.

I slide and step my way through and over branches and broken particle board until the debris opens up into just thousands of shards of broken glass on the floor and take my first look around the destroyed atrium. Even as I'm cursing what they've done to us, I have to marvel at the brilliance of their plan. It probably took next to no effort to down the two huge trees right on to the building, destroying any chance we might have had of using this place long-term. I don't even know if our plants will be salvageable with so much glass everywhere. If we do try and pick what we've grown so far it will have to be done extremely carefully.

I don't see any soldiers in the destruction but what I do see has me cursing full out. There's a smoldering fire with wisps of smoke on the other side of a tangle of bent ceiling beams. I'm looking for a way through the mess to get to it and put it out when a breeze blows through the now shattered windows and it flares to life. If I could get to it in the next few minutes, I might be able to put it out, but I can't find a way around or through the mess between me and it. In the time that I take to look for a way through, the fire grows enough that I know there's no way I'm going to be able to put it out.

These frackers didn't just plan on taking us out and stealing our supplies. They wanted to completely annihilate us. I curse again at the stupid short-sightedness of it. Why they would want to burn this place down when there's so much in it they could have used themselves is beyond me but it doesn't matter now what their motives were. They're dead and we need to get out of here.

I pick my way back through the debris and branches, weaving and bobbing until I make it through and back into the hallway. I rush to the clinic door where Joslin is standing, look past her into the room at Ethan, Marsh and the two scared faces of the boys. I hate that Ben and Matty had to go through this but there's no time to deal with it right now.

"Time to go! Ethan, you're going to have to grab everything you can from in here and stuff it in a bag. They started a fire in the atrium and it's growing. Joslin and I will get Marsh up and moving toward the front of the building if you can grab some supplies and bring the boys."

He has a brief look of panic across his face as he glances around the clinic he worked so hard to set up but it changes to resignation and he nods his head before leaning over Marsh. He starts tapping his son's cheeks to get him to wake up. When his eyes flutter open I see them dart around the room in confusion before he sits straight up with a cry of pain and anguish twists his features. Ethan puts a steadying hand on his shoulder.

'Whoa there, just take it easy, Marsh. Do you remember what happened?"

As Marsh tries to come up with some clarity, Ethan motions Joslin over to take his place. When she has a firm hold on Marsh to keep him sitting, he pulls out a couple of syringes and two vials of medicine from one of the drawers. While I wait for them to get moving I send a quick glance down the hallway but there's still no sign of smoke so I go into the clinic to help. While Ethan is loading up syringes and injecting Marsh, I grab a couple of bags and start emptying drawers into them. Whatever Ethan injects Marsh with works fairly quickly because his trademark goofy grin spreads across his face and silliness spills from his mouth.

"Yogi Bear got caught in a trap! But I didn't get any pic-a-nic-a baskets," he says in a weird voice.

Joslin shakes her head in astonishment and looks to Ethan. "What the heck did you give him? He's high as a kite!"

Ethan nods and throws the syringes away before taking one of the bags from my hand and starts adding supplies to it.

"Yes, morphine will do that to a person but more importantly, you can move him now without him screaming in agony. You'll need to support him on both sides. Take him down to the dining room and get him up on a table for now. We should have a little bit of time before the fire gets there and we have to abandon the building completely."

Joslin and I get a shoulder underneath each of Marsh's arms and we slide him over the edge of the table onto his one good foot. We shuffle slowly toward the clinic door and I glance over my shoulder at Ben and Matty where they're still sitting on the floor in the corner and send them a reassuring smile. I'm about to tell them to stay put until Ethan says it's time to go when pounding footsteps can be heard in the hallway and Rex starts yelling.

"Skylar! Matty…Sky?"

That's all Matty needs to hear to launch himself to his feet and dart around me through the door. I really don't want Ben to see the dead bodies in the hallway but it looks like that's a lost cause when he tries to dart around me too. I reach out with my one free hand and snag him by the back collar of his shirt before he can make it to the doorway. I pull him back until he's at my side and I glared down at him sternly.

"Where do you think you're going? Two minutes ago there was a gun battle out there! You honestly think it's safe just to run out like that?" When his face shifts to fear I pull him closer to my side and soften my tone. "I think it's over but you have to listen to me when I tell you what to do. I'm trying to keep you safe, Ben. If you want to be treated like a big kid then you need to act like one and that means following orders in an emergency."

Marsh takes that opportunity to slide into the conversation. "Yeah, Benny, man - you got to put your big boy pants on now!" he said, followed up with hysterical giggles.

I just ignore him and motion ahead with my chin now that I don't have any free arms. "All right, let's go. But Ben, you stay right here beside me the whole way. And just so you know, there's three people out there who died and it's not pretty so try and keep your eyes looking up at the ceiling until we get into the dining room, okay?"

He nods hesitantly at me with a trembling mouth but takes a step toward the door so Joslin and I start moving again. We've barely made it into the hallway when Rex practically runs right into us. I blow out a frustrated breath at all these delays but the fear on Rex's face has me pushing my frustration to the side. I let go of Ben to hold up a hand to get him to stop.

"We're okay! I cleared the atrium and there's no one back there so unless you guys found any other soldiers outside, I think we're clear. Ethan's just packing up what he can from the clinic. We have to get out of the building! There's a fire in the atrium and it's not going to take long for it to spread to the rest of this place. We were just headed down to the dining room. If you can take Marsh the rest of the way then Joslin and I can go check on Belle and Sasha and start grabbing some of the food before we lose it all."

He looks past me in the direction of the atrium before nodding his head in agreement and slipping in underneath Marsh's arm to take my place. He looks down at his brother.

"Matty you and Ben go with Skylar and Joslin and help them start packing up some of the food. I'm right behind you guys." He has no problem supporting Marsh on one side and he glances over his shoulder into the clinic and yells at Ethan.

"Come on! You're never going to be able to bring it all. What you have is good enough! We need to move to the front of the building before the fire starts spreading down this way."

He must get an agreement from Ethan but I don't stick around to find out. I grab Benny and lift him up onto my hip, forcing his face into the crook of my neck so he won't see the bodies that I navigate around. I go past Jackson sideways so there's no chance that Ben will see his blank staring eyes and slide into the dining room. Joslin's right behind me with Matty and we settle them at a table at the front of the room without a view of the hallway. I rush into the kitchen and look every which way for Belle and Sasha but there's no sign of them so I just start yelling.

"Belle! Belle!...Sasha! Are you guys in here?"

There's a creak of a door opening so I spin around and see Belle peeking out of the pantry with a scared expression on her face. I try really hard not to be annoyed that she and her daughter have hidden away in here while the rest of us were out there fighting for our lives. I understand that they're not fighters but I'm also just a seventeen-year-old girl who shot at least three people today. I give her a hard look and wave her the rest of the way out of the pantry.

"You can come out now, it's safe. The good news is, the rest of us took care of the bad guys. The bad news is, the building is on fire and we need to grab as much of our supplies as we can and get out! So, if you're done cowering in the corner maybe you could help us with that."

I turn on my heel and walk out of the kitchen, I have no patience right now for her excuses. I might be being unfair to them but it's hard to be objective when they hid, leaving Ben and Matty and the rest of us to deal with this. The boys are still sitting at a table in the corner waiting for me while Rex and Joslin are sliding Marsh onto a table. Rex looks up at me with a questioning expression.

"They're fine, not a scratch on them. I found them hiding in the pantry." I turn away from him toward the other end of the dining area where we've stacked all the empty bins we had originally brought all the supplies in. "I'm going to grab some bins and start clearing shelves into them if you guys want to grab a few and help me."

With my arms full of empty bins, I'm halfway back to the kitchen door when Lance and Ethan come into the dining room. Ethan rushes straight to Marsh and checks the bandages on his leg and Lance takes a moment to look around the room at all the faces staring back at him. He lands on Joslin and strides over to her putting both his hands on her shoulders.

"Joslin, I am so sorry about Jackson. I wish I could have been in here to help him."

Her face crumples in grief for a moment but then she smoothes her expression out to her normal calm demeanor. "Thank you, Lance, but there was nothing anybody could have done to stop what happened there. Right now, we need to focus on getting as much stuff as we can out into the yard before the fire reaches here."

He studies her for a moment before finally nodding and dropping his hands from her shoulders.

He turns and looks at the rest of us around the room. "Joslin's right, we need to try and salvage as much as we can and get it out into the yard. We can load everything up onto the trucks once the fire forces us from getting anything else. We don't have much time so we need to get moving."

Belle, clutching Sasha to her side, looks around the room frantically. "Why do we have to load it on the trucks? Where would we go? We decided to stay here for the winter!"

I walk over to her and shove the stack of bins against her until she's forced to take them from me. "We can't stay here, Belle. This building is going to burn to the ground and most likely the fire will spread to the other structures, if not to the forest behind us. It's not safe for us to stay here anymore. We don't have any choice. We have to go!" I say in exasperation.

Lance tries to calm her down. "It's okay, Belle, we'll figure it out. As long as everyone's safe, we'll be okay. Right now, I just need you to focus on getting as many of the supplies out before the fire reaches here. I promise we will find a new home that's just as good as this one."

I go back over to the wall and grab another stack of bins when Belle replies.

"Sasha and I don't want to go to the city. We don't even know if it's safe there!"

I turn away from the wall with the new bins in my hands and head toward the kitchen again. I sent her and Sasha a dark look filled with impatience.

"We're not going to the city. Marsh needs proper medical facilities for that leg. We're going back to the bunker. Now move your fracking butts and start helping!"

Chapter Twenty - Joslin

The room erupts with questions and denials at Skylar's declaration of our destination but she just sails past everybody and disappears into the kitchen leaving them all to turn to me with their questions. I throw my hands up in the air.

"Stop! We'll discuss this once we've gotten the supplies outside. Now is not the time for this. Everybody needs to get moving!"

I make my point by rushing over to the stacks of bins and grabbing a few before running into the kitchen. Skylar is not even trying to pack anything neatly, she's just using her arm to sweep items off of shelves into her bins so I mimic her actions and do the same. The truth is if we're headed back to the bunker we really don't need all of these supplies. In this world though, it just feels wrong not to try and salvage as much as we can. She looks over at me as we work and shakes her head.

"Man, this is so déjà vu! In a way, it feels like yesterday when Belle, Sasha and I did this exact same thing in my own pantry when we left the bunker. I can't believe we're going back." When I don't reply she moves closer to me. "I know now is not really the time to deal but are you okay? I mean... Jackson?"

I bite down hard on my lip when I feel the emotion surge up again. She's right about this not being the time to deal with my grief. We need to just focus on what we're doing here. They'll be time later to grieve properly for my best friend so I give her a small nod and turn away from her compassionate eyes.

Rex, Belle, and Sasha come into the kitchen with bins and start emptying out the fridge and freezers but no one speaks as we all pack as fast as we can. I try and think of everything else we should try and salvage besides the food but I doubt we will be able to get at anything else from the back of the building at this point. I know it's stupid to feel sad about material possessions when Jackson has just died but it's easier to be sad about losing all the things Skylar and I had shopped for at the resort then it is thinking of never seeing or speaking to him again.

Once all of my bins have been filled, I carry the first filled one out of the kitchen past the others and into the dining room. The little boys, Marsh, Ethan, and Lance are gone so I assume that they've all moved out into the yard and head that way. When I enter the hallway I look toward the atrium where smoke is now starting to billow around the branches and debris blocking it. I turn away from it and head toward the front door when it's pulled open and Lance strides in and takes the bin from me.

"We've got Marsh set up in the yard by the playground and the boys are watching over him. Just start leaving the bins here in the hall and Ethan and I will haul them out for you guys."

I'm about to turn back to the dining room when a scary thought occurs to me and I quickly turn back to him.

"Are you sure you got them all? I mean the soldiers? I heard the one say that they had been staying in the resort and that they were watching us for the past few days. Is there any chance that one of them stayed back and is still a threat to us?"

His face freezes for a moment at this bit of information but then he shakes his head.

"I doubt it. We outnumbered them so there's no way they would have left back anybody who could have fought on their side. Most likely, they figured they could take us out with fewer numbers being trained soldiers. But I am willing to bet they left at least a few guys back at the growing fields to control the people they're holding there as slaves. We can talk about it once we're done clearing the building but for right now I think the threat is over."

I take his word for it and we both turn to go our separate ways, him outside to deposit the bin in the yard and me back to the kitchen, but my steps slow before I enter the dining room and I looked down the hall at where my room is. I know it's selfish but I just can't help myself from running the rest of the way and throwing open the door to my room. The smoke is starting to get thicker in this area but the heat hasn't made it this far so I know I have at least a couple of minutes to grab a few things. These belongings mean more to me than just the stuff that they are. These things were the first belongings that I owned that I picked out and that I loved and got to keep. Selfish or not, I'm going to hold on to that and take as many of them with me as I can. I grab a few of the boutique bags and start stuffing as much as I can into them of random things around the room. I let myself take three bags of clothing and knick-knacks before grabbing my backpack and stuffing it with as much of the tech that I had brought from the bunker as I can fit into it. When I start coughing from the smoke that's filling the room, I know my time is up and I grab the handles of the bags and dash back out and down the hallway to the yard. I drop my bags beside a growing pile of bins and let my lungs suck in the clean air for a few seconds before turning around and heading back in.

It takes us five more trips to get all the bins that we're going to get out into the yard before the smoke is too thick for us to chance going back in. The last thing Rex and Lance carry out is Jackson's body. They carry him over to the big tree in the corner and lay him down on the grass underneath it before coming back to join the rest of us where we're sprawled out in the yard around the bins and trying to catch our breath from the smoke inhalation.

Everyone keeps sending looks toward Skylar and me but I'm not quite ready to have that conversation yet so I walk over to the old hand pump and get it going to fill the bucket we leave out here. Once it's filled I set it aside to douse my head completely under the cold water to try and wash away the ugly smell of smoke that's clinging to me. I wring my hair out and slick it back from my face, then lug the heavy pail of water over to the others so that they can drink or clean up with it and finally go and sit down beside Marsh. I pick up his hand and hold it in mine, taking comfort from the warmth of it. The morphine must have knocked him back out again but I feel a slight tug on my lips when I see that even in sleep, he has that goofy grin on his face that I love so much.

I sit there and watch the fire consume the building we had planned on making our home in and just let the flames hypnotize me into an emotionless state. One by one, everyone comes and settles in a circle around Marsh. Ethan leans over and takes

Marsh's other hand and checks his pulse. Once he's satisfied with what he finds, he sets his son's hand gently back onto his stomach and sits back.

Lance coughs a few times to clear his throat, breaking the hypnotic daze I'm in. I glance his way to see him looking at Skylar. She's got a faraway expression on her face as Ben cuddles against her but she focuses on him when he addresses her.

"Skylar, I think you better explain to us why you think we can go back to the bunker. We were all there when AIRIA counted down her self-destruction. Do you know of another way to get into the bunker? And do we even want to go back there with no power or water?"

Skylar sighs deeply and plants a kiss on Ben's head then looks around at everyone waiting for her answer.

"AIRIA didn't self-destruct. We don't know how she managed to get around the virus Joslin uploaded into her coding but our best guess is she just did a reset to before the General took control of her. She's up and running."

Belle leans forward and practically snarls at Skylar. "Do you mean to tell us, that all this time, we could have gone back to the bunker and lived safe and comfortable inside of it? How dare you keep this from us?"

I stare at her in surprise. This is new. I've never seen this ugly side of Belle before. I look over to Skylar and see the heat building in her eyes and wait for the fireworks to go off but Lance intervenes.

"Belle!" he says sharply, "What are you doing? If Skylar had information about AIRIA and the bunker it's her information, not ours. She doesn't owe us anything when it comes to that place!"

His words do nothing to soften Belle's features or tone. "Like hell she doesn't! We're supposed to be a group. We're supposed to work together and share everything. Isn't that what you said? Don't you think we should have been told if we didn't have to be out here all this time? None of this would have happened, we could have been safe in the bunker if she had just spoken up."

Skylar laughs but there's no humor in it. "Oh yeah, we're a group all right, when it suits you! Tell me Belle, where were you today when there was work to be done? When Lance, Rex and I were out here where the bullets were flying, where were you and your daughter? Were you working as a group to help protect the children? Were you working as a group to help Ethan with Marsh? No! You and your daughter hid in a cupboard while the rest of us risked OUR LIVES to protect yours! Lady, I don't owe you anything! And I'll tell you another thing, we might be going back to the bunker but it won't be permanent.

We'll go back there and spend the winter but come spring, everybody's out! I don't give a damn where you and Sasha go but I'm going outside to start rebuilding this world because I won't spend the rest of my life inside that mountain."

I turn to look at Belle and Sasha. Sasha hasn't said a word since we came out here, she's just staring down into her lap with tears dripping down her face. Belle has the decency to look chastised by Skylar's words and she seems to realize that she's overstepped in her demands by her contrite expression. It's an interesting dynamic that hasn't really played out before in this group. If these two can't come to some sort of agreement, it's going to be a very long winter.

I turn away from them to Lance for his reaction and see him staring at Belle with a look of disappointment on his face before he shakes his head and turns to Skylar to say something to her but then changes his mind and looks at me instead.

"Joslin, you're the tech guru here so please tell me, are you sure AIRIA is functioning? If we head west back to the bunker, we will be using up precious gas that we can't spare if for some reason we get there and we can't get in."

I shrug a shoulder. "No, I don't know for sure. We'll have to dig up the communicator that Skylar buried to check before we go anywhere. Hopefully, it still has a bit of a charge left in the batteries so we can know for sure if AIRIA responds to us or to Skylar. If she reset back to before the General took control of her, then she probably wouldn't respond to me at all."

He nods and switches his focus back to Skylar. "Okay, so where did you bury the communicator then?"

Skylar winces and shoots me an apologetic glance before answering him. "It's buried underneath where you put Jackson."

Lance looks over his shoulder in that direction with a sad face.

"Um, that was where we were planning on burying Jackson, if that's okay, Joslin? I thought it would make a nice spot for his resting place."

I nod my head in agreement. "I think he'd like that. In the sun but shaded by that pretty tree is a lovely spot. If you don't mind I think I'll just stay here with Marsh while you guys do that."

His tone is sympathetic and understanding. "Of course, stay here and we'll take care of everything. I'll come and get you when it's time to say goodbye."

I don't reply, just look down at Marsh's hand in mine. Skylar, Rex, Ethan, and Lance head over to the tree that Jackson is laid out under and Belle and Sasha get up and go to their cabin to start packing up their belongings. Ben and Matty go sit on the swings and talk quietly to each other leaving Marsh and me alone. His hand squeezes in mine alerting me to the fact that he's woken up and my eyes meet his bright blue ones. They're a little hazy and cloudy but they're looking straight at me.

"Who are you saying goodbye to?" he asks in a raspy voice.

He winces in pain when he tries to sit up on his own so I quickly move to support him in a seated position and wonder if I should call Ethan back to give him some more painkillers. He's still looking at me waiting for an answer but it's hard for me to say the words out loud so I clear my throat a few times and finally push it out.

"Jackson. I'm saying goodbye to Jackson because he died today."

Confusion fills his eyes and he turns his head to look around the yard and then zeros in on the main building.

"How long was I out? The building's on fire!" He turns panicked eyes at me. "What happened Jos? Is everybody else okay?"

I nod my head and rub his back to reassure him that his family and friends are fine. "What's the last thing you remember?"

His brow furrows in thought. "I want to say something about Yogi Bear but I'm pretty sure that's not right…There was a trap! I stepped into a trap and… That's it. That's the last thing I remember."

"Okay, well here's the quick and dirty of it," I begin. "You stepped into a very nasty bear trap that was put out deliberately to injure us by one of the General's soldiers. They tracked us here from the growing fields after we drove past them on the way back from getting the stoves. Apparently, they've been hiding out in the resort watching us for the past few days. We don't know how many times they came over the wall before today but we're guessing that they are responsible for the missing chickens and the fire that took out the generator and the fuel. Jackson and Rex got you back inside the gate and while Ethan was working on patching you up, the soldiers managed to topple at least two of the old trees behind the atrium just outside the fence so they both crashed through the glass ceiling and part way into the building. After that, they attacked us and there was a gun battle out here that Lance, Skylar, and Rex fought. One of the soldiers made it inside but Jackson and him shot it out…killing them both." I suck in a breath to help keep my tears at bay and go on. "When Skylar checked the atrium, she found that one of them had set a slow burn fire but before she could get to it to put it out it flared up and took hold. We grabbed as much as we could and evacuated to out here." At his shocked expression I nod slowly. "So yeah, that happened. Oh, and apparently AIRIA is up and functioning too so we're going to go back to the bunker for the winter. That wraps up the events of the past hour which is roughly how long you've been out of it." I lean back as exhaustion fills me.

He shifts his wounded leg with a grimace and then rubs at his forehead. "Wow, I know I said I was a champion napper but sleeping through all that? I really am!"

A half laugh escapes me. "Sorry buddy, you can't take all the credit for it. You had a little bit of assistance from your new friend, morphine."

"Ah, now the Yogi Bear thing makes sense!" The humor drains from his face and he pulls me closer to him. "So, Jackson? I'm so sorry, Jos. I know how much he meant to you. I'm here whenever you want to talk about it but I understand if you're going to need some time to process it."

I smile at him in gratitude. "Thank you, Marsh. When I'm ready... Until then you need to focus on healing and getting better. The good news is, going back to the bunker means Ethan will have a proper clinic with an x-ray and everything he needs to speed your recovery."

His grin slides across his face. "And unlimited hot showers again?"

I shake my head with a laugh. "Yes, and unlimited hot showers again."

Chapter Twenty-One - Skylar

Before we grab some shovels to start digging Jackson's grave, the four of us make a circuit around the burning building to look for any signs that it's spreading out to the other structures. The heat from the blaze keeps us well back, but thankfully there's hardly even a breeze today so it shouldn't spread too far within the camp. The biggest concern after that is it spreading to the forest itself. The two huge trees the soldiers toppled onto the building, which also took down a good portion of the fence, are leaning against the atrium side of the building giving the fire a straight path of fuel toward the forest. After talking it over we decide we can't let that happen if at all possible. So instead of grabbing the shovels to start digging, we grab the two chainsaws that we had brought over from the resort and use some of our precious gas to fill them up. The best we're going to be able to do is cut the two trees and part of the log fence on either side of the building and pull it all away from the fire.

It's back-breaking work in the heat from the sun and the fires, plus the smoke clings to everything and fills our lungs. It takes two long miserable hours to get the debris cut down to manageable sizes before Lance can bring the tractor around the outside of the fence with the plow attachment on it to dig a trench between where the fence once was and where the tree line begins. It's all we can manage with the equipment and manpower that we have.

The four of us are filthy, completely exhausted and worn right out from a day that never seems to end coupled with the previous night's lack of sleep due to the generator and gas fire. All I want to do is throw myself down on the grass and sleep for a few hours but we still need to dig Jackson's grave and retrieve my buried communicator. I know if I stop now I'm not going to get started again so I just swap out the chainsaw for a shovel and head toward the old tree in the corner.

I look over at the playground where I last saw Ben and Matty playing and I'm relieved to see Joslin has them both seated at one of the picnic tables with some food. Not that long ago, I was the only person in Ben's life who could take care of him so I'm grateful for the people around me, even Belle and Sasha, at odds or not.

When I reach the tree I stare down at Jackson and let the guilt I've been keeping at bay flood through me. I was unfair to him this morning when I doubted his place in the group and practically accused him of setting the fire. I wish now I had gone back and apologized to him for the way I treated him. He was probably just trying to find his way like the rest of us. It was taking him a little bit longer and I let my impatience and frustration get the best of me with how I treated him. I'll never get the chance now to really get to know him. The guilt of that is something I'm going to have to live with for a very long time, especially knowing that he lost his life defending the ones I love the most from his father's soldiers.

A crash breaks me from these thoughts causing me to spin around quickly to see where it came from. The fire has finally consumed the entire building and the roof is falling in on itself. I turn away from the senseless loss of our home and gently reach down and shift Jackson a few feet away from where I need to start digging. The shovel bites into the dirt easily and it only takes me a few minutes to dig down far enough to where I buried the decorative box containing my communicator. I pull it free from the dirt and brush it off before setting it off to the side unopened. It doesn't feel right to open it and check the communicator to see where we'll be spending the future months while Jackson is waiting to be put to rest. The shovel bites into the ground again and again until my shoulders and arms ache. I lose myself in the labor and repetitiveness of it so much that I'm not even aware when Rex, Ethan, and Lance show up with shovels of their own and start digging beside me.

Rex's hand on my shoulder jolts me back to the present and I turned to face him.

"Sky, did you hear me? I said that's deep enough."

I nod my head in weary understanding and reach up my hand so that he can help me out of the hole. I roll my head around on my neck to try and get some of the kinks out before driving my shovel into the ground to keep it upright and look to Lance and Ethan.

"I'm going to go douse myself under the hand pump for a few minutes if that's okay? I'm feeling a little foggy. I need a bit of a wake-up."

Ethan's eyes look incredibly sad as he stares down into the empty grave that's waiting for his apprentice but he nods anyway.

"Of course, Skylar. Go and get cleaned up and then if you don't mind let the others know we're ready over here, please."

I squeeze his arm to try and give him a little bit of comfort at his loss and then turn and scoop up the decorative box and carry it with me over to the hand pump. I don't even worry about how many people are in the yard or how many eyes might be looking my way when I whip off my shirt. The sports bra I'm wearing underneath it covers the same amount of skin as a swimsuit top and I need to get the sticky, sweaty shirt that reeks of dirt, smoke, and sweat off of me for a few minutes. I get down on my knees and let the cold water wash away the grime, stress, and exhaustion of the last twenty-four hours. The freezing water also helps numb some of the painful emotions that keep flooding in and out of me. Even under the hot sun the cold water eventually makes me start shivering and I have to shut the flow off and move away from the puddle I've created. I just kneel there with my eyes closed and my face up to the sun letting its warmth dry some of the water dripping off of me until a shadow blocks its light. I open my eyes to see Rex standing in front of me with a soft smile on his face and a towel and shirt in his hands for me. I let him pull me to my feet and then use the towel to dry off before accepting the shirt and sliding it over my still damp skin. His smile turns to a frown.

"I just realized, you lost all your stuff, Sky. You didn't have a chance to grab anything from yours or the boy's rooms before the fire reached it, did you?"

I shrug my shoulders. "It's just stuff. I can always find more. The most important thing is no one got hurt." I wince at that, thinking of Jackson. "I mean, no one got hurt in the fire that is."

He nods understandingly at me. "Yeah, I know what you mean. Everyone's ready to say goodbye to Jackson if you're ready?"

I look away for a second to gather myself and then nod to him and take his arm. We join the others who are standing around the open grave. Jackson is resting at the bottom of it with his arms crossed over his chest and he looks peaceful for the first time since I met him. Ben comes to stand beside me and takes my hand in his, looking up at me with a sad expression on his little face. I have no words to comfort him right now but we will have a conversation after the service so I can try and help him make sense of this tragedy.

Ethan clears his throat and all of our eyes turn to him.

"I only knew Jackson for short time but in the time we had together I came to respect and admire him greatly. He was a smart, strong, compassionate young man who was working hard to overcome the damage his father and those he was surrounded by inflicted upon him for so many years. He wanted nothing more than to learn how to heal people and he eagerly absorbed all I could teach him about being a doctor. It saddens me immensely that he'll never get the opportunity now to apply those skills to try and make this world a better place."

Ethan falls silent and looks toward Joslin. Her eyes are glued to the bottom of the grave and when the silence lengthens she lifts them to look up at all of us before sighing and wiping a tear that's trickling down her face away.

"Jackson and I became friends before the bombs dropped when I dumped a bowl of spaghetti over his head in the middle of our school cafeteria after he had bullied me. I have no idea why he chose to become my friend after I did that but from then on, he was always by my side. He saved my life the day most of the world died by standing up to his father and insisting that I come with them. He had the biggest heart. No matter how often his father would put him down or talk down to him or dismiss him, he still tried everything he could to please him and to gain his love. That man was unworthy of Jackson's loyalty and love. In the end, he chose me again and helped us secure this place with the supplies we needed to thrive here. He gave his life to protect me and the others in that building against his father's evil followers. I wish he was still here to see how we're going to rebuild and change this world into a better place but I'm grateful for the time he did get to spend here with us. He got to see what it means to be a part of a real family and for that I'll be forever grateful."

She turns away from the grave and picks up a shovel and then scoops up some dirt and lets it rain down gently into the hole. "Goodbye Jackson. Thank you for being my friend and my family."

Lance has been supporting Marsh next to her and he reaches out and places a hand on her shoulder. "Joslin, again, I'm so sorry for your loss. Why don't you help Marsh back over to the picnic table and we will take care of the rest of this."

She nods gratefully at him, passes off the shovel and then gets an arm around Marsh's waist to help him hobble back to the picnic tables. I can see how much pain they're both in. Him, physical and her, mental. It makes my heart ache for them both. When I drop Benny's hand and move to get a shovel of my own, Rex waves me off.

"We've got this, Sky. Why don't you take the boys over as well and try and get something to eat. We'll have a meeting once we're done here."

I send the boys ahead of me back to the picnic tables and go back over to where I've left the box with my communicator beside the water pump and retrieve it. While I'm over in that area, I take a few minutes to check on the chickens and Nods. She's come through the drama of the last day unscathed but I can tell by her pacing around in her enclosure that she still filled with anxiety. Between the multiple fires, the smoke that fills the air with a haze, and the gunfire that filled the yard a few hours ago, she must have been in a full-blown panic and we'll be lucky if she doesn't lose the calf growing inside her big belly from the stress. I take the time to just stand and brush her coat for a few minutes and let her press her big flat head against my chest like she does when she wants love. She seems to be calmer by the time I turn and head over to the picnic tables and I have to smile at my crazy cow that acts more like a dog than anything else.

When I get to the picnic tables I can tell just how shaken up the two boys are by their lack of chatter. They're both just sitting staring at the wooden table top picking away at a few splinters but not speaking. I slide onto the bench beside Ben and reach my arm around him to pull Matty even closer to us. I know how hard this is for me to process the ups and downs of something always going wrong so it must be even harder for them. All I can do is reassure them that we're going to be okay and hope that once we get back to the bunker, we'll have an uneventful winter with some sort of normal life for both of them.

Belle and Sasha sit down across from us and Belle reaches across the table to put a hand on my arm.

"Skylar, I want to apologize to you for how I acted earlier. You were right, my first instinct was to take Sasha and hide in the pantry when the gunfire started. I'm not going to apologize for doing that but I will promise you that I will work on changing that reaction for any possible future encounters. It isn't fair for Sasha and me to expect you and the others to do all of the hard work of keeping us safe and secure. Sasha and I will train more with all of you on firearms and try to do better. As for what I said about the bunker and you not telling us about it, I was flat-out wrong and for that I do apologize.

"When the bombs dropped, we were stuck in the storage room with Rex and Matty for over two weeks and I had time to process what was happening. When Marsh and Lance found us there and took us in, we stayed in the same house for seven years and we managed to have some sort of life together there under the radar. When we were forced to move from there to the hotel, it seemed like minutes later things started going wrong and they've just kept going wrong. From going to the bunker to leaving the bunker to coming here and now going somewhere else again. Apparently, I'm not very good with change. Since we left the place we called home for seven years, it's been crisis after crisis and constant upheaval. I hit my breaking point with this last attack and I reacted badly," she says and laughs softly at herself. "I guess what I'm trying to say, is that sometimes I don't react well to new things, but that's also something I'm going to try and work hard on, to be better at."

I glance over at Sasha and meet her eyes. She nods her head in agreement with her mother's words but her apology takes me by surprise.

"I'm sorry too. I wish I was more like you, Sky! You're so strong and you don't even think twice about rushing into a fight. I just don't have that kind of bravery. I've never needed to have that. Lance, Ethan, Rex, and Marsh have always done the dangerous work for our group. They've always protected us but if you'll help me, I'd really like to learn how to protect myself. I hope you can help me be brave."

I stare at her in astonishment. I don't even know how to take that. I don't feel brave! I don't feel strong most of the time. When these stupid incidents happen all I really feel is mad. I just take that mad and channel it into actions. At a loss for words, I just give them both smiles and nods. Thankfully, the men join us right then, saving me from having to fumble out some type of explanation. With two picnic tables pushed together there's room for all of us to sit. The box with the communicator inside of it is sitting in front of me and Lance points to it.

"All right, I guess before we start making plans for where we're going next, we should see if that thing really works. Skylar, open it up."

I look at all the faces surrounding me, watching the box expectantly, and blow out a breath. I flick the latch holding the lid closed and pop it open. Inside is a plastic zip baggie with the communicator inside of it. I pull it out, open the bag, remove the device and flick the power button on. My shoulders slump in frustration when nothing happens.

I look over at Lance and shake my head. "Sorry, dead battery!"

Before he can respond, Joslin reaches over and plucks the communicator from my hands. She pushes up from the table and swings her legs over the bench.

"No problem. I have a couple of power packs in one of the backpacks I managed to get out of my room. It'll just take a few minutes to get enough of a charge into it to turn it on."

Lance rubs at his face tiredly and looks back at us. "All right, while we're waiting for that thing to power up let's go over some of our options again. With the bunker possibly back in play, the city no longer looks all that attractive to me. At least, not until the spring that is. If we can get back into the bunker, it makes more sense for us to winter there where we have plenty of supplies and there's room to grow food. The question I have for all of you is, what do we do about all of the people the soldiers are holding hostage down at the growing fields?" When no one replies right away he goes on. "I think all of our first knee-jerk reactions would be, not our problem but I think we should look at this long-term. I agree with Skylar about not spending the rest of our lives in that mountain, as comfortable as it may be. If we truly want to start rebuilding things out here then we're going to need more numbers. We now have only eight adults in our group and that severely limits what we will have the capacity to do. Look what happened here, we didn't have enough people to set a permanent guard watch and now we've lost the place. That was just trying to manage this small camp, but if we're going to look at planting more crops, raising more livestock and making homes that are livable and survivable for all seasons then we're going to need a lot more people."

He pauses when Joslin comes back and sits down, placing the communicator and the connected battery pack in the middle of the table.

"I'm guessing that the majority of the people that they have down there are ones who had spent time inside the bunker with us before the General showed up," Lance continued. "There's probably also quite a few who managed to get away from them scattered around in this area and in Canmore. If we do nothing and leave them alone, there's a very good chance the majority of them will not survive the winter and then if we're going to look for more people to join our community we will be forced to look further away. Who knows what type of people we will find out there? So, I want to hear everyone's opinion on this. More people or no people?"

He starts it off by pointing at Ethan.

"More people," he says. "We can't truly rebuild anything unless we're willing to start by rebuilding relationships with other survivors."

He moves on to Rex who responds with, "More people."

Marsh says, "The more the merrier!"

He points at me and I just shrug. "Sure. Mi casa es su casa," I say in a deadpan voice. When Lance just cocks his head at me and lifts his eyebrows, I nod quickly. "No really, I mean it. You're right, there's no way we can make very much progress with just eight functioning adults. I'm on board with that."

When his finger swings to Ben and Matty they both bounce in their seats excitedly shouting "More, more, more!", causing everyone to laugh.

Sasha just nods her head and Belle says, "Of course we will help them."

Joslin is the last of us to be polled and of course, she goes all analytical on us. "In regards to housing more people inside the barracks, there's sufficient supplies there to support upwards to a thousand people for five years minimum. As far as a workforce goes for the future, we would most definitely need to add personnel to the community in order to make any real progress toward re-establishing a pre-bombing civilization. Even adding considerably to our numbers it will still take us years if not decades to get anywhere close to where we were on the day of the bombs. Realistically, it will take more than one generation to get to that point."

When we all just stare at her, she shrugs her shoulders. "Yeah, that means more people."

Marsh leans toward her and nudges her shoulder with his own. "That's my girl! So sexy when you sound like a robot."

Her head whips around and she glares at him. "You're lucky you're injured or I'd punch you for saying that!" she says, then she leans over and plants a kiss on his cheek to soften her tone.

Lance rolls his eyes at their antics and says, "Right then. So, that's a unanimous agreement that Marsh doesn't get more morphine because it makes him stupid. Also, yes to rescuing the people being held at the growing fields and looking around to recruit others to join us. I think that's the best choice we could make at this point. There was a time to hide to survive but that time is over now. But not today. Today, we go and get settled somewhere else, whether it's back at the bunker or just over to the resort next door for now. It's been a very long night and an even longer day today and we all need to take a breather before we do anything else." He looks down at the communicator on the table and then up at Joslin.

"Is that thing charged enough to turn on yet?"

Before she can answer him I snag it and pull it toward me. I flip the power switch and feel a small thrill go through me when the green light comes on. I hold down the transmit button and almost breathe out my question.

"AIRIA? Are you there?"

The sweetest words flood back toward me from the speakers

"Skylar Ross, how may I be of service?"

Chapter Twenty-Two - Skylar

Now that we know the bunker will be our next destination, everyone relaxes a little bit or as much as we can with a building on fire across from us and the grief of losing Jackson still so fresh. Lance and Rex take the pickup truck over to the resort to scout it out and make sure that there were no soldiers left behind there that will be a threat to us.

While they're gone, I round up everyone else except for Marsh, he's dozing on one of the picnic tables after a second injection of painkillers from his dad. We get as many buckets and containers as we can and fill them with water from the hand pump and then dump them all around the perimeter of the burning building to try and contain any sparks so the fire won't spread. Once we've completely saturated the ground all the way around the building I want nothing more than to go into one of the cabins and crawl into a bunk and pass out. It's not on the agenda for a few more hours sadly. Even though we lost a lot of our supplies in the fire and we're going to a bunker filled with inventory, there still a lot of things that we don't want to leave here in the cabins that we need to pack up to take back with us.

The stack of bins sitting in the middle of the yard that we had managed to get out of the main building need to be loaded into the cargo truck so I send the two younger boys over to feed the animals while Joslin, Ethan and I start lifting them into the back of the truck. Belle and Sasha go from cabin to cabin and pull out everything that needs to be packed as well - piling those items in the center of the yard with the rest of the bins.

Once we've managed to put everything into the back of the truck I turn and survey the yard of the camp with my hands on my hips. I let out an exhausted groan when I realize how much more work we have ahead of us before we can quit for the day. Joslin looks my way at the noise so I just point at what made me groan.

She follows my finger with her eyes and it makes her own loud groan. "Oh my God, we can't leave that, right? We're going to have to harvest the whole garden, aren't we?"

I decide to just lower myself down to the ground and sit for a few minutes while I think about that and she settles down beside me and passes me a canteen of water. I take a deep drink of the tepid water and look longingly over at the hand pump where I know crisp, cool water is waiting for me but I just don't have the energy even to crawl that way. Instead, I just let the almost warm water slide down my throat before answering her question.

"Well, not all of it's really ready to be harvested yet and we no longer have any containers that we can transfer them into because they were all in the atrium. We put an awful lot of work into getting the garden set up and growing, so as much as I would love to just turn my back on it, we're going to have to pull as much as we can. Even half grown fresh vegetables are better than no vegetables."

She glances over to the playground where Ben and Matty are playing and then looks back at me with a mean expression on her face.

"If we're rebuilding civilization then we're going to need new laws. I vote that the first new law we create is to bring back child labor! Let's make the monkey's pull all the vegetables! Can I get a second on that vote? Please, pretty please?"

We both crack up with laughter and once I've caught my breath, I add to her dream. "Yes and while we're at, can we get a waiter over here with dinner and a tall drink filled with ice cubes please?"

Her eyes go big. "Oh yes, that's what I want and also a masseuse. I've never even had a massage before! I want someone to come and rub my feet and I'm willing to tip big for it!"

I laugh at her expression of longing and glance over at where Marsh is dozing. "Well, I think you might be in the market for that now. Think about how he can't run away for at least a month. You could turn him into your foot rubbing slave."

Her eyes get even bigger and her cheeks flush bright red when she chokes out my name. "Skylar!" That causes me to laugh even harder.

Lance and Rex drive back into the yard just then and Rex comes over and stands above us where we're sprawled out on the grass giggling. He looks from Joslin to me and shakes his head with a smile.

"What are you guys doing?"

I flutter my eyelashes at him and say in a haughty tone, "We are waiting on the waiter to bring us our dinner and drinks!"

Joslin rolls over onto her side and braces her head on her hand before saying in the same tone, "I have a spa appointment that I'm waiting on."

Rex's smile grows even larger at our silliness. "Huh, and here I was thinking you girls were working hard."

Joslin looks up at him and says, "We are working hard. We were also developing new laws for our new civilization. Law number one was just voted in with overwhelming support!"

Rex drops down to the grass between us and leans back on the heels of his hands. "Really? And what was law number one?"

I roll over until I can rest my head in his lap and look up at him. "We voted to bring back child labor so that we can make the monkeys pull all the vegetables from the garden and then do anything else we want our little minions to do."

He barks out a laugh and then looks at us incredulously. "Do neither of you remember what happened the last time you asked the boys to weed the garden?"

Visions of newly grown baby vegetable plants ripped from the rows and thrown in the weed pile dance through my head causing me to pretend sob.

"The monsters! They killed so many baby carrot plants!"

I lift my head from Rex's lap and push myself into it a seated position before getting onto my knees and up on my feet. I reach down and pull Joslin up as well and take her by the shoulders and give her a serious look.

"He's right, the staff here is completely unreliable! The waiter isn't coming and the spa just burned down. We're going to have to do this ourselves. Brace yourself, we can do it!"

She shakes her head with a grim expression. "Fine, we'll do it ourselves but I'm leaving a one-star Yelp review on this place before we go!"

We both crack up again and stagger our way toward the garden and the next few hours of work ahead of us.

Everyone pitches in to harvest the garden and other than loading the animals up in the morning we're ready to leave. My stomach rumbles reminding me that I've barely eaten anything today and I look around the yard trying to figure out how we can make some food out here. All of our cooking utensils, pots, and pans were destroyed in the fire and judging by the lack of bins left out we've packed all the food as well. I look up into the sky and judge that we still have three or four hours of light left and then look around at all my exhausted friends and family. We had planned to spend the night here and then head to the bunker in the morning but it seems stupid not to just go now. It'll mean another hour of work getting the livestock trailer hooked up and the animals loaded into it but I think it's worth it for a hot shower, hot food and a soft bed to sleep on tonight.

I take my idea over to Lance who just stares at me blankly from where he's sitting at one of the picnic table benches but then he nods and pushes himself to his feet. He turns to the others that are sprawled around the area.

"She's right," he says tiredly. "I'd kill for a hot shower right now. Everybody up, let's go home."

I know it's the right call when everyone except for Marsh pushes to their feet and moves toward the cabin with the chickens. Benny comes over to me and tugs on my shirt until I look down at him.

"Are we really going home, Sky?" When I nod my head at him his expression shifts from excitement to concern and he asks me, "Are we going to have to be stuck inside again? I really like being outside now."

I pull him against me and plant a kiss on the top of his head. "No, we won't be stuck inside ever again. I promise we will be able to go outside whenever you want. This winter when it snows, you and I are going out and we're going to make the biggest snowman you've ever seen."

He pushes away from me and does the funky little happy dance before whooping and dashing in the direction that Matty went before he screeches to a halt and turns back toward me, his little face is filled with confusion.

"What's a snowman?"

I shake my head with a laugh and shoo him away and as tired as I am, my heart feels light. I'm going to be able to give my boy the best of both worlds now.

It only actually takes us half an hour to get the trailer hooked up and the animals loaded with everybody pitching in to help. When we drive through the gates of the camp, I don't look back. This isn't an ending, it's the beginning of something else instead. I don't know where we will be in the spring or who all will be with us but I do know this is the first step toward a renewal of all the things that we've lost. And I know that I won't ever stop fighting to give Ben a better life. After so many years of doing it alone, I now know that with family at my back, we can do anything.

Read on for a peek at Land – the first book in the Stranded series!

Land, A Stranded Novel - Prologue

"So much blood, how can there be so much blood?" was all she could think.

She just wanted to go home. She was only seventeen, just a kid. It wasn't fair. She had been hung from a wall to be raped. She had shot and killed people and now she was supposed to perform surgery on one of her best friends. Why did this have to happen to her? She just wanted her mom and dad. She wanted to go home.

When her sobs subsided, she stood back up and looked out over the fields. The voice behind her didn't jolt her but the words did.

"There's a reason why we all think you should be the one to do this, Alex. You're our leader. You always have been. Right back to when we were kids and you marched us into the forest and bossed us around to build our clubhouse. You've always taken the lead. Quinn might be the responsible one but you are our glue. It was always you that held us together and organized all the adventures growing up. You have the biggest heart and you are one of the strongest people I know." He gave a small laugh. "I wasn't surprised a bit when you came through that door at the biker's house. I knew you'd find a way to get free. You're a hero, Alex. We trust you to do this."

Alex shook her head in denial. "I'm scared out of my mind, Josh! I'm not a hero!"

He smiled a compassionate smile. "Don't you know, Alex? That's what a hero is. Someone who's scared out of their mind and does it anyway." He opened his arms wide and she rushed into them. He held her tight and said no more.

Sign up to my newsletter to be notified of new releases and special discounted prices.

Please visit: http://theresashaver.com

Also by Theresa Shaver

The Stranded Series

Land – A Stranded Novel, Book One

Alex, Quinn, Josh, Cooper and Dara - setting out on foot with nothing more than some soon to be worthless cash and a little advice from a trusted teacher, they walk through a burning city that has come to a halt. The devastation they see as they make their way out of the city is a small part of the horror that the nation will become. As the days go by with no food deliveries and no water flowing from taps, civilization will start to crumble and it will be survival of the fittest. With five States and half a Province to cross they will need to plan well, count on each other and pray for a little luck. Even with that, chances are slim of getting home when you are Stranded.

Sea – A Stranded Novel, Book Two

Emily and her friends head to the California coast to find a boat back to Canada. They all felt that it would be much easier and quicker to sail home rather than go over land. They were wrong. Not only will they have to fight their way through the lawless city and the terrifying ocean, they will have a journey of hardship and loss as the biggest threat will come from within their own group. The trip home will change them all for good and bad as they are stranded at SEA.

Home - A Stranded Novel, Book Three

Five went by Land and five went by Sea. Nine made it through the chaos Home. With their town under siege, and their families both prisoners and slaves, they will have the biggest challenge yet. After witnessing the pain and suffering in the town, the group of teens has to decide just how far they are willing to go to save them. Life sucks when you are 'Home', but still Stranded.

City Escape – A Stranded Novel, Book Four

Mrs. Moore and the rest of the students that remained in California face the harsh reality that no one is coming to help them. As the city burns around them, they are surrounded by 18 million people with one goal...survival. Will Mrs. Moore's determination be enough to save them? Surrounded by chaos, they must work together to find a shelter before it's too late.

Frozen – A Stranded Novel Book Five

When the teen's town is hit with a devastating virus, they take it upon themselves to travel first to the closest military encampment to find the medicine their loved ones so desperately need. Stonewalled at every turn they make the hard decision to embark on an epic journey to a faraway city to search the ruins for help they need.

Traveling through a Frozen wasteland, they not only have to fight the elements and other survivors but also the inner struggles and changes each one has to accept and live with.
It's not just the weather that has Frozen.

Iced – A Stranded Novel, Book Six

The sixth and final book in the Stranded Series sees the teens injured and divided. With Alex out of commission with her injury and seven small kids to protect, Quinn is forced to keep them hidden and protected at the hospital while hoping they won't be discovered by more of the sick scavengers that attacked them. Josh and the rest of the group have the challenges of negotiating a deal to relocate the nurse and terminally ill children to the zoo. If successful, they still have to attempt to reach the medical supply depot for the medication their town desperately needs. All while avoiding the gangs that rule the inner-city core. The clock is ticking against them as the Chinook weather front can end at any moment leaving them all ICED in place.

<u>The Endless Winter Series</u>

Snow and Ash – An Endless Winter Novel, Book One

Bomb after bomb dropped across the globe sending the world into a seemingly never-ending nuclear winter.

Skylar Ross is ten that day when she's ripped from dance classes and sleepovers to being an orphan in a prepper's paradise of a mountain bunker. Her determination to protect her baby brother keeps her locked away with nothing but responsibility and loneliness. Her father's words are a continuous echo, "Trust no one. Help no one."

Rex Larson is eleven that day. He's left stranded on the side of the road in a strange place far from home when his mother dies that first day. With his own small brother to look after, he is lost and alone. Rex has no choice but to trust complete strangers with his and his brother's future.

Two different survivors in two different circumstances spend the next seven years trying to survive until an explosive meeting changes both their courses and lives forever. Trust is almost impossible when you spend your whole life in the SNOW & ASH.

Rain and Ruin – An Endless Winter Novel, Book Two

A hailstorm of bombs has blasted the world into a nuclear winter. The survivors have now spent seven long years in the snow and ash scratching out a lonely, hard existence.

Although comfortable in her safe and supplied bunker, Skylar Ross longed for more of a life than what she has. She thought she found it when she rescued Rex but the evil that followed him inside her home threatened the one person she holds most dear. Can she put aside her mistrust of others and give him and his people a second chance?

Rex Larson fell hard for Skylar and was excited about his group joining her in the safety of her bunker until he was betrayed by one of his own. Exiled back out into the cold, he prays that Skylar will change her mind.

Forced to flee the town when a deadly gang moves in, the survivors huddle in the cold hoping the gang won't find them and for Skylar to change her mind. When the weather turns for the first time in seven years, they don't know if it means the earth is starting to heal or if it's just more ruin.

Sun and Smoke – An Endless Winter Novel, Book Three

Skylar Ross and Rex Larson just settled into a new way of life when a simple mistake changes everything. General Bill Mallor, Skylar's Godfather, should have been a welcome sight when he and his men roll into town and save them. Instead, he becomes her biggest threat and enemy when he snatches control of AIRIA and evicts her from the only home she knows. She has to come to grips with the fact that she's just a powerless teenager with no weapons. She has no hope of beating him.

Joslin Frost should have died with everyone else the day the bombs dropped, but the General's son dragged her into a bunker. Thrown into a war, she experiences the hellish nightmare of the lower levels of AIRIA East. She survives by hiding and becoming a ghost.

Her hatred for the General has her playing the long game to bring the great man down. She's a teenager just like Skylar but she's not powerless and she has the biggest weapon of all…the truth.

Fire and Fury – An Endless Winter Novel, Book Four

AIRIA is dead. The bunker is shut down.

Skylar, her friends, and family lost their home in the bunker when the General and his men took control.

Joslin, working as a double agent on the inside, took the General down, freeing Skylar and the others. The cost was high with the loss of AIRIA and access to the bunker and all its supplies.

Forced to create a new home under the now clear sky is both a blessing and a curse for Skylar.

Navigating new and old relationships to build a community is a challenge she hopes she's up to. Life in the summer camp Joslin found for them seems too good to be true as they build and grow all they will need to thrive. Skylar settles in, coming to realize the difference between existing inside the mountain and living under the sky and swears she'll never go back. She should have known it wouldn't be that easy to start over in the apocalypse.

As new relationships form and old ones fray inside the community, an enemy they thought they were free from waits on the outside for the right moment to strike.

The Flare Series

The Journey – A Flare Novel, Book One

What would a mother endure to reach her children in a catastrophic global event?

What would she let stand in her way to reach them?

Nothing…nothing would stop her.

Lila Duncan is months away from leaving her husband and setting up a new happier home for her kids. Freedom is so close she can almost taste it. While attending a conference almost 400 miles from home to help reach her goal, the unthinkable happens. A massive Solar Flare hits the planet wiping out all modern electronics including all modes of transportation. The world begins to burn as civilization is stopped in its tracks.

Frantic with worry for her son and daughter in the care of their indifferent father, she decides to tackle the journey home on foot. Between her and home are the Rocky Mountains that she will have to cross.

The Journey will take every ounce of will and determination she has but not even a mountain range can compete against a mother's love.

The Line – A Flare Novel, Book Two

What would a mother be willing to do to rescue her children?

What Line would she cross to find and protect them?

All of them...she would cross all the lines.

Lila Duncan fought her way over the Rocky Mountains to get back to her kids. She made it through the gruelling elevation changes of the mountains. Pushed through the injuries she sustained from her accident. Lived to tell the tale of a grizzly bear encounter and escaped from a raging forest fire to make it home.

Finding her kids missing and her home empty, Lila now has to change from being just a determined mother to something else. She will need to be a soldier, a mercenary, and be willing to cross any Line to get them back because she has to face her biggest challenge so far...a city that has descended into madness.

The Bridge – A Flare Novel, Book Three

What would a mother do to give her kids peace and safety in a dangerous new world?

What bridges will she be willing to build to make that happen?

Build them or burn them, she would do anything for her kid's future.

All Lila wants to do is get her kids far away from the city to her father's farm where they can rest and be safe from the chaos that has consumed the world. She is shocked beyond belief by the changes he's made to the property since she was last there for her mother's funeral. Not only has her childhood home been completely changed but she arrives just as an old feud is kicked up into an all-out war.

There are family and community bridges that she will have to build and if that doesn't work, she'll not only set them on fire, she'll blow the damn things up!

Scorched – A Dry Earth Novel

All choices lead to death when the sun has Scorched the world.

Claudia has never seen rain or any water that hasn't come from the old well behind her house. Now the well's about played out and today they closed down the ration stations, for good. The gangs are circling to rob and loot the little they have. Her only choices are to go north to the slave labor camps or stay and die by the gangs.

Her grandmother wants them to run south and follow an old map that will lead them to a secret valley with all the water they will ever need. She swears it's there but how can she drag her nine-year-old sister and an eighty-year-old woman out into the desert wasteland that surrounds them based on an old map?

Enjoy this clean, stand-alone adventure novel that moves at a fast pace!